Dark Secrets

Erica Frost

Published by Erica Frost, 2022.

DARK SECRETS

First edition. December 2, 2022.

Copyright © 2022 Erica Frost.

ISBN: 979-8223033059

Written by Erica Frost.

Table of Contents

Dark Secrets
New Adult Enemies to Lovers Romance

By: Erica Frost

Foreword

Secrets are to be protected. Especially when they're dark.

Gabriel Price thinks he has it all. Bad boys like that always do. But, he can't have me. Not as easily as he thinks, at least. Avoiding him on college campus is mission impossible, and finally I give in. After all, what's the harm in one date?

Fate laughs in my face, as the enemy becomes the lover. How cliché. We're drawn to each other like magnets, but it seems the closer we get, the more dangerous our lives become. I feel like someone's out to get me... or maybe someone is just trying to catch my attention the wrong way?

They say you can't run away from the sins of your fathers. If only I knew this before...

Dark Secrets

Chapter One

Ava

I've never felt more of an ugly duckling than now, elbowed and pushed by all these duck-pouting, chest-flaunting girls who tried to find their way through a bustling bar filled with college kids. My hair isn't nicely pressed, fresh out of the salon, nor are my clothes screaming modern fashion trends. This t-shirt is second-hand, so are the jeans. My hair is an uncombed mess. My face is cleanliness embodied. No makeup.

All I can do is sigh, because Sylvia, my roommate, will not let me go home, not until I've had at least three cocktails. Her words, not mine. I glance at my drink, half-gone. It's only the first one.

"The night's still young," Sylvia notices me watching it sorrowfully.

Her pink hair stands in stark contrast to her black t-shirt and the chains around her neck. Someone once told her she looked like someone's dog that got lost. While the guy was still in the middle of talking, she curled her fist and punched him so hard, she broke his nose. That was the last time someone compared her to a dog, just because of the choice of necklaces she prefers.

"I feel like I'm ancient," I tell her, forced to lean closer to her, because I doubt she can hear me from the loud music.

"You're an old soul," she smiles at me sympathetically. "Stuck in a young woman's body. That's a tough combination. But you still gotta drink three cocktails. That's you ticket home."

"Expensive," I chuckle. "Are you sleeping over at Chad's?"

She frowns but doesn't reply. They probably argued again, which is nothing new. Sylvia says arguing so much makes their make up sex a hundred times better. I wonder if it's worth to argue just for the sex. Sylvia would reply affirmatively to this, I'm sure.

"Not tonight," she shakes her head, and a few strands of her pink hair get stuck to the corner of her equally pink lips. "It's just him and his hand tonight. That's his punishment."

I roll my eyes, still smiling. "You guys are impossible."

"Hey, you have to let them know who's boss," she shrugs, raising her glass and urging me to take another sip. I oblige, although a little reluctantly. I try to remind myself that the sooner I get this over with, the sooner I'll be back in my bed.

Suddenly, an explosion of laughter spills all around us, managing to outweigh even the loud music. Sylvia and I look over in that direction. Everyone does the same. I roll my eyes, only this time I don't smile.

"Gabriel Price," Sylvia says his name out loud, as if we don't know who he is. "He's hot. I'd fuck him."

"Sylvia," I frown, although I still keep looking in his direction. It's hard to look away. He's one of those guys whose magnetism is too powerful for its own good.

"What?" Sylvia shrugs. "You'd fuck him, too. You just don't want to admit it."

"I do not," I knit my eyebrows more forcefully this time. Whether I'm lying or not, doesn't really matter.

He's got a glass of beer in one hand, and there are two girls on his left, fighting for the privilege to hang off ofoff his arm. The usual kind, big lips, big tits, small brain. I wonder if whether they're even from around here, or if whether someone brought them over for some fun. I bite my lower lip, reminding myself that this was mean. Girls should stick together, not being bring each other down, just for the way they like to dress.

"I need to go to the bathroom," she informs me, placing her glass on the bar, right by mine. "You OK staying here on your own?"

"Yes," I nod, although I am filled with dread at the thought. Not because I'm afraid that someone will start hitting on me. That happens rarely, and I know it's because I seem aloof. I seem like I'm not even having fun being here, so why would anyone approach someone who's the epitome of a party-pooper? No. It's because a part of me is afraid that I will drown in this cacophony of phony sounds and people.

I sigh silently, watching Sylvia disappear in the sea of people. I try to focus on the music, but the rhythm is difficult to catch or understand. Maybe Sylvia is right. Maybe I really am an old soul trapped in a young woman's body. I watch as other people have fun, dancing, drinking, talking. A part of me wants to join in, yet another part of me wants to forget about this whole nonsense and just go back to my room.

I grab my drink and down the final two gulps. Alright. That's one down, two more to go. I gesture at the bartender to send us a round, when suddenly, I feel someone's light touch on my bare elbow.

"Well, finally, I thought someone snatched you on your way to the– " That's "That's as much as I'm about to say before I realize that it's not Sylvia touching me at all. It's Mr. Hot Pants.

"You could snatch me if you want," he flashes me a row of pearly whites aligned to perfection. I wonder if they're even his real teeth or he had them fixed. It wouldn't be unheard of.

It takes me a moment to process what he just told me. A wary silence crackles in the air between us, suffocated by the sound of music.

"Do I know you?" I ask, knitting my eyebrows at him.

This takes him off guard, and he tries not to let it show. "Everyone does."

"I'm not everyone," I shrug.

"I've noticed."

Dammit, he's smooth. I try to remind myself that he's a player. A bad boy. The baddest of the bad boys. But it's hard to focus on that when's he's looking so fine.

"That's why I came over."

"Aw, you shouldn't have... Gunther, is it?" I flash my eyes at him, knowing this will probably rub him the wrong way. He frowns, doesn't say anything. "Sorry, it's Gunner, right?"

"Close," he seems amused at this point. "How many names you got starting with G?"

"As many as you'd like," I reply. "Grayson. Gerald. Gatlin. Granger. Now, if you've got European roots, you might be Giovanni, Gilberto, Giancarlo..."

"OK, OK," he chuckles. I reluctantly agree he's even more handsome when he's amused. "You're good with names. Now, if you only knew mine."

"I know the ones that matter," I shrug, turning away from him and grabbing my drink.

"Let me buy you another one," he offers, eyeing my colorful cocktail with a red umbrella and a little sweetened cherry.

"Thanks, I'm good," I shake my head, taking a little sip. "By the way, my friend will be coming back soon. She'll need her spot back."

"I can keep it warm for her until she comes back," he grins again.

Dammit. Dammit it to hell.

At that moment, a tidal wave of people seems to push back at us, and the girl standing next to me lunges right into me, making me spill my colorful cocktail... right onto the Grecian god before me. My hands open to his chest. I can feel his chiseled body through the wetness of his shirt, and I immediately pull back as if singed.

"Oh, God..." My brows furrow as I watch the hippie tie die explode on his chest and his white shirt. "That won't wash off."

He looks down, and bursts into laughter. "This? It's fine. You can always get me a new one, if it doesn't wash off."

"Me?" I send him a look of daggers. "It was an accident."

"Even in an accident, someone is to blame."

"Not always," I correct him. "Sometimes, it's just a sequence of unfortunate events, and no one is really to blame."

"Yet, a shirt is irreparably ruined," he gestures at his chest, and a part of me wants to press my open palms to him once again... just for the heck of it.

"You've got money, just buy another one," I say a little more spitefully than I plan on.

He doesn't get offended. It's the opposite, his eyes widen, and he smirks.

"So, you do know who I am?"

Dammit. Dammit to hell.

"Gabriel," I admit finally.

"Good girl," he snickers.

"Not for you," I snarl back.

"I love girls with some spunk."

"I thought you like easy girls."

No. No. No. I keep revealing how much I know about him.

"Eh now," he clicks his upper lip with his tongue. "There are no easy or difficult girls. It's just a matter of who wants what, and eventually, finding the right person to provide that for you."

"I can't provide anything for you, I'm afraid," I immediately say. "And that's my friend right over there."

I point at Sylvia who's on her way to us, but the moment she notices who I'm talking to, she stops and turns to the side, chatting up a guy standing right next to her. And just like that, I'm on my own again.

"Seems like she's found a distraction," Gabriel pinpoints the obvious.

"Great," I down the rest of my drink in one thirsty gulp. "Then, I can also call it a night. Goodbye."

"Wait," he says, his fingers grabbing my elbow gently, but with enough force to make me stop. "Can I have your number?"

I give him a dirty look. "Seriously?"

"Yeah," he nods.

"Not a million years," I pull my hand away from him, and walk over to Sylvia to tell her that my first night out in the last six months has been exactly as I imagined it: slightly awkward, slightly painful, and slightly dizzy.

Sylvia, the good friend that she is, comes back home with me, and we quickly fall asleep, after I am forced to give her an update on what me and the Golden Boy were talking about.

The following morning, she barges into my room, carrying her phone in it.

"Ava, Ava!" she shouts louder than anyone is supposed to shout on a Sunday morning. "Wake up, you gotta see this!"

"Where's the fire?" I mumble, trying to hide underneath the covers, but she pulls them off ofoff me.

"Look," she urges, shoving the phone right in my face. The light almost blinds me.

I rub my eyes sleepily, then try to focus my gaze on the phone. I'm surprised to see myself in the photo Sylvia is showing me. Next to me, I see him, Gabriel, just when he was holding me by the elbow. We look so close, almost intimate, as we're staring each other in the eyes. My lips are parted. I'm looking up as if I'm mesmerized by him, expecting him to kiss me any moment. If I ever find out who took that damn photo, I'm gonna break their phone.

"What?" I jump from the bed, grabbing the phone from her hand. "Who took this?"

"I don't know," she shrugs. "Someone from his crowd."

"But, why?"

Then, I see it. He even captioned the photo.

You owe me a new shirt or a drink. You choose.

"Ava..." Sylvia's eyes widen in shock upon realizing what just happened. "Is Gabriel Price inviting you out?"

I swallow heavily, all the little hairs on my body standing on end.

"Seems so," I grimace. "But what I want to know is why?"

Chapter Two

Gabriel

"We on for beers tonight?" Brandon asks, as we throw ball in the vast greenery on the campus. We still have two hours before the next lecture, and a few of us decided to hang out a little.

"Sure," I nod, as I follow the ball with my gaze, catching it right in my hands.

I look to the side. Ashley is pouting at me, and I know what that means. It tough when you used to hook up with someone from your own crowd, but then decided to stop it. Sometimes, the other side just won't take no for an answer.

I guess it's my fault, too, because while I don't want to be with her, she sometimes invites me over and I don't say no to just a quickie or even a night of casual sex. It's the no after that which she takes a bit too personally. I look away from her, not wanting to give her too much attention. She always takes it the wrong way. Brandon tells me I should consider myself goddamn lucky, because she's one of the hottest girls around. She's even smart. So, according to Brandon, she's the whole package. Only, it's not the package I'm after right now. Not that I'm even looking for packages right now.

We throw ball for a while longer, when suddenly, he throws it over my head. I turn around and I see her. The girl from the bar, the one that spilled her drink on my white shirt. I hear Brandon saying something, but I'm paying no attention to him. That night from last weekend rushes at me, reminding me of the thrill of the chase. How she tried her best to show that she has no idea who I am, or that she's interested in talking to me. She's made me work for it. I've been trying to find her, at the same time, trying to make it appear the opposite. The Insta post was meant to provoke her, but it didn't. I guess it wasn't enough. I don't remember the last time I had to chase a girl. It's all gotten so easy, too easy.

There she is now. Right here. Walking quickly, rushing with a book pressed to her chest. Her curls are bouncing as she's walking, a flowery dress fluttering around her ankles. It's the grandma length, Brandon would say. Not short enough to provoke attention or interest, and not long enough to do the same, by making you employ your imagination. Usually, I agree. Not this time, though. It looks so effortless on her, as if she just stepped out of the fifties, and knows that she's completely different from everyone here, but doesn't give two shits about it.

I'm barely registering what Brandon is shouting at me. I throw the ball back in his direction quickly, without aiming properly, then run after her. It doesn't take me long to catch up with her, stopping right before her, so she can't go past me.

One look at her, and adrenaline hits me like a ton of bricks. That petite body, that fierceness in her eyes, those locks...

"You're in my way," she says instead of a hello. Not that I expected her to say it.

"You haven't responded to my Insta."

"What?" She knits her eyebrows again like she did that night. Her nose scrunches up a little.

"The photo?" I remind her. There isn't a flicker of recognition on her face.

"I haven't seen it," she shrugs. "I don't have Instagram."

"Seriously?" I raise my eyebrow at her. It's almost unbelievable that someone in this day and age doesn't have Insta, or any other social network profile.

"Seriously," she confirms, looking fidgety, as if she wants to be anywhere else but here. "Even if I did have it, I probably wouldn't respond to it. No offense."

She disarms me completely. It is so easy to flirt with other girls because they make it so easy. I don't even have to try that hard with jokes. Whatever I say, they find funny. She on the other hand, isn't like that. With her, I try to speak, and I fail miserably, and it's both pissing me off and making me try harder.

"Non None taken," I say the first thing that pops to mind. "I still think you owe me a drink or a shirt."

"You want me to take you on a date to make up for the shirt I've ruined?" She sums it up pretty well, although her face is completely expressionless.

"Well... yeah," I grin, scratching the back of my neck a little nervously. Maybe I shouldn't have done it in public like this.

"But we can't stand each other."

"We can't?" I frown. "Says who?"

I huff at her suggestion. She can't possibly mean that. She doesn't even know me. How can she not stand me? I'm used to girls knowing me, liking me before knowing me even. The uncertainty on her face is palpable.

"Says my gut feeling," she tells me.

"What if your gut feeling is wrong?"

"It's rarely wrong."

"Can I prove it wrong?"

She sighs. That's strike two, I'd say. One more, and I'm out.

"Look," she starts, sounding exhausted by the conversation, and dammit, that's making me even more confident that I want to make her change her mind. "I'm not the type of girl you usually go out with. Just stick with your comfort zone, OK?"

My comfort zone? The whole campus is my comfort zone!

She's trying to confuse me, but she won't.

"Maybe it's you who's afraid to go out of your comfort zone," I tell her.

Her eyes meet mine suddenly, unexpectedly. They are a pale green, with golden frames. Firecrackers explode somewhere inside my head, as my gaze clings to hers. She refuses to look away first. So do I. I watch the rest of her face with the corner of my eye. Her skin is like porcelain, framed by the copper sheen of her curls around her face.

"Everything is out of my comfort zone," she finally says, suppressing a chuckle. "So, if you were trying to dare me to do something, good luck with that."

I grin at that. "How do you feel about bets?"

"Bets?"

"Yeah," I nod. "Give me a condition. If I make it, you have to let me take you out. If not, I won't bother you ever again. What do you say?"

She thinks about it for a moment or two, then nods. There is a mischievous glimmer in her eyes, and it suits her perfectly.

"How are you with philosophy?" she asks.

I frown. "Uhm, not very good. Why?"

"Great," she smiles. She shoves the book she's holding right into my hands. "Here."

"What is this?" I wonder, looking at the book.

"It's Nietzsche," she says nonchalantly. "You do know who he was, right?"

"A philosopher?" I've heard of him. There was this meme Brandon sent me once.

"Bingo," she nods. "There is a quote I like very much. I'm not upset that you lied to me, I'm upset that from now on I can't believe you."

"But I didn't lie to you."

This time, she chuckles loudly, melodiously, with her entire face lighting up. "That's the quote."

"Oh," I smile back, wishing that she remained in that blissfully smiling state forever.

"Find that quote in this book."

I glance at the book. It's not that short, but I've seen worse. Haven't read it, but I've seen it. This should be a piece of cake.

"Sure, should I call you when I find it or what?"

"No," she shakes her head. "I'm going to get a cup of coffee, and I'll be back here in an hour. If you've found it by then, I'll go out with you. I'll even pay for the drink."

"An hour?" I ask, incredulous. "Is that even possible?"

"Depends on how fast you read," she shrugs, taking a step to the side, then passing me by. "Remember, an hour."

With those words, she starts walking, leaving me alone with the book. Still bewildered, I look at what she's left me with. An hour for a whole book? That's crazy talk. That's... undoable. Clarity finally sinks in. She's given me an impossible task, knowing I won't be able to do it, just so she wouldn't have to go out with me.

I should just leave it be. I shouldn't even bother with this book.

At that moment, I feel someone tug at my elbow. A familiar perfume scent fills my nostrils.

"Hey, babe," Ashley purrs in my ear.

She is pressing against me, and I can feel the softness of her plump breasts against my upper arm. I expect to get aroused immediately, but strangely, nothing happens.

"We still have some time," she whispers, and I know what she's insinuating. It wouldn't be the first time that we have sex in her dorm room, my car or even one of the nearby café's bathrooms. We could totally do it. I need something to distract me from this girl who thinks she's too good for me. What better distraction than a quickie?

Yet, my main man won't spring into action, even when she gently brushes her upper thigh against it. Nothing. Absolutely no reaction to her closeness, to her suggestion, to the fact that her tits are right there for the taking. Nothing.

I know she'd rock my world during those few minutes of sex. She'd be exactly the kind of distraction I'm looking for, and yet, I don't want it.

"Can't," I pull away from her magnetic hug, and I can't fail to see the look of surprise on her face.

This time, she really thought I'd agree to it. I did last time, although I also promised myself I wouldn't. But how can you say no to something that's been shoved right in your face? Somehow, I can say no now.

"Need to check something in this book," I show her what I'm holding in my hands. She's still speechless. Maybe it's the rejection, maybe it's the fact that I'll be reading a book when no one is making me do it. That's not the image I want to project: one that I like books. It's hard enough hiding that part of myself.

I remind myself that I don't have to do this. It's a stupid bet. That girl knows I can't do it. That girl? It only hits me then that I don't know her name. If I don't read this stupid book and find the quote, she won't tell me.

I don't even care. Why should I care about her name at all? She's shown me where she stands. Maybe I should just count my losses and go sink into Ashley's warm—

"Hello?" Ashley waves her hand in front of me. "Earth to Gabriel?"

"Sorry," I shake my head. "Got lost."

"I can see," she's pulled away from me. I can tell she's hurt. Maybe even a little insulted.

"I'll see you later," I tell her, glancing at Brandon who seems equally lost. I wave at him, showing him the book. He still doesn't get it.

Neither do I. Still, I rush after the girl, in the direction of the café. It's the closest one. I can only assume she's headed there.

Why are you even doing this? I hear that little voice of reason. It's asking the right questions, as always. I could have stayed with Ashley. I should have stayed. I would have had a good time, and my day would be just like any other day. That phrase rings inside my mind. Just like any other day. I realize I don't want that. I want a different day. But to have a different day, you need to do something different. Something drastically different.

So, I hasten my step hoping that I'll catch the philosopher girl before she's out of the café.

Chapter Three

Ava

I'm seated by the window this time. I'm looking out, through the people passing by. I see a few familiar faces, but I don't wave, even if they look in my direction. I never wave. I've never been a social butterfly, and that hasn't changed with me starting college. I've always preferred books and closed doors to outings and big groups of people. It's not that they frighten me or make me uncomfortable. It's something else. Something far more crimplingcrippling, and that's the fact that you're always afraid that you'll do something stupid, something that will follow you for the rest of your time there.

I still remember the banana peel incident back in high school. I was just minding my business, the first day of the first week. The cafeteria was crammed with students. Then one of the cool girls threw a banana peel onto the ground right as I was passing by. I slipped on it, fell and every single bit of the food on my tray ended up on my face and in my hair. My mom said she never knew how difficult it was to get coleslaw out of your hair. Well, now we both know. And it's something neither of us want to repeat ever again. Why did the girl to do that to me? Just because. Mean people don't need a reason to be mean. They just are. And they are usually also very popular for some reason. It's a twisted world we live in. And I will have no part in it, ifit if I can help it.

Suddenly, someone slumps into the seat opposite me, and slams the book onto the table in front of us. I look at him, shocked to see Gabriel.

"Only ten minutes have passed," he tells me, immediately opening the book. "I decided I wanted to do it in front of you, so you know I'm not cheating or anything, and that I'll win this date fair and square." He says it so quickly, not even lifting his gaze to meet mine. He's already started reading, his finger trailing the lines. I don't interrupt him.

The quote I've given him is somewhere on the hundredth page, more or less. If he reads just slightly faster than the norm, he should be able to find it in time. Or, if he knows how to skin skim through books, which is also a skill applicable only to those who have read hundreds of books in their lifetime. I don't want to stereotype him, but he was probably a cool jock in high school, something that hasn't changed in college, and I doubt he did any of his homework. Some poor nerd must have been doing them it for him. That's just how things go, I guess.

I keep my gaze averted from him as he reads. I'm looking out of the window, squeezing the cup of coffee in both my hands. A part of me regrets just not telling him no. But that's another thing introverts are very bad at, refusing people thing, even if that refusal comes at the cost of something dear or valuable to themselves. For example, this date will cost me my precious time. As Sylvia would say, yes, he's handsome, but I haven't seen much charm from him yet. He's full of himself. He thinks girls should just throw themselves at him, and I guess that is what's driving me away the most. He's not even trying that much.

I sneak a peek at him. OK. He's more than just handsome. His hair is slid to the side, with a few stray hairs falling over his forehead as he leans over my book. He's wearing a white, short-sleeved t-shirt this time, and I can see the veins underneath his skin tightening. He's not only drop dead gorgeous, he's in shape, too. The whole package. But all that's physical. Being pretty means nothing. Pretty people are usually more shallowshallower than a puddle after rain.

I have no idea how much time has passed. I dare not call him out that an hour has elapsed, when I haven't checked the start. I sigh silently, figuring I'll wait another fifteen minutes and then just call it. I won't be sitting here all afternoon, waiting for him.

"There!" He exclaims importantly, his index finger pressing down at the book, in the middle of the page. "I found it."

There is a victorious gleam in his eyes, as he turns the book around to face me, so I can read it. I don't need to. I only glance at the page, and I know he's found it.

"It's been over an hour," I say, surprising even myself with what a sore loser I am.

"No, it hasn't," he corrects me, showing me his Jaeger LeCoultre watch. "Exactly fifty-three minutes have passed since you gave me your instructions and conditions. I have met them."

I bite the inside of my lower lip nervously. I don't want to go on a date with him. All he will probably do is just talk about himself. That's not how I want to spend a whole hour or even more, and I sure as hell don't want to give him any hope of landing me in bed.

"I honestly wasn't expecting you to do it," I admit.

"I know," he grins. "I used that for extra motivation."

I almost chuckle out loud, but instead I just smile.

"That's what I'd like you to wear for our date."

"This?" I look down at my dress. It's nice, but nothing special.

"No, that," he points at my face. "Your smile."

Dammit. I forgot how smooth he was. But I won't fall for this.

"Alright," I admit. "I've lost fair and square, as you said. I agree to a date with you. One hour. One coffee. One time."

"I agree with the first two, this time," he corrects me. "That final one is up for discussion."

"It's a non-negotiable offer," I say.

"I'm good under pressure," he grins again. "How about we do it now?"

"Now?" I repeat, not expecting his suggestion.

"Sure," he shrugs. "We're here, the two of us. I've got exactly one hour before my next lecture, so you know I won't keep you any longer than you've stated. What do you say?"

I look around, realizing that he might have a point. We're already here. I lost that bet. Prolonging this will just make it more annoying.

"OK," I sigh.

"You look like someone just told you that your kitty died," he tells me.

I almost feel like that, too. But I don't say that.

"What can I get you?" I ask. "I owe you a drink for the shirt, no?"

"No, it'll be my treat this time."

"No," I shake my head, getting up. "My treat. Americano?"

"What are you having?"

"A mochaccino."

He replies without even thinking about his answer. "I'll have the same."

I nod, and after a few minutes I return with a mochaccino for him. I'm still wondering whether this is a good idea or not. What the heck. I'm here. Let's just get this out of the way.

"Thanks," he says, taking it into his hands. His fingers are long, bony somehow. He's got big hands. Sylvia has a naughty saying about men with big hands.

"Just so you know, we're not considering this a date," I say, wanting to clarify.

"No?" He asks, seeming amused.

"No," I confirm. "It's just two friends having a coffee."

"So, we're friends now?"

Dammit. Here comes that smooth player again. I have to keep reminding myself that it's easy to fall in this trap.

"I'd say we're acquaintances," I correct him, taking a sip of my coffee, staring at him from the rim of my cup. He's not taking his eyes off ofoff me. I suppose I cold could be accused of the same.

"That's a good start," he grins.

"Now, honestly," I suddenly say. "Have you ever read anything by Nietzsche?"

"Honestly?" He repeats. I nod. "No."

"I appreciate the honesty," I smile. If I have to sit here for an hour, maybe it couldn't hurt to actually try to be nice to him.

"I prefer Kierkegaard," he says, and my jaw almost drops. I think it's noticeable, because he continues. "What? You thought I was just a stupid jock?"

"Honestly?" I use his words this time. He nods. "Yes."

"Well, I can't blame you," he shrugs. "Although it's not nice to stereotype people."

I'd hate to admit it, but he's right. Still, maybe this is just him pulling stuff out of some invisible hat in an effort to wow me. I'm curious to see whether he actually knows anything about Kierkegaard.

"So, why do you prefer Kierkegaard to Nietzsche?" I wonder. "They're both existentialists, after all."

He lifts his eyebrow at me, as if it was his turn to be wowed.

"I think that Kierkegaard anticipated modernism, you know, the individual choice behavior."

"And Nietzsche anticipated the perspectivism of post-modernism," I add.

"Yeah, they say he was inspired by fascism," he adds. "I don't like that."

"He was also inspired by the ideas of self-liberation and authentic expression. He urged for the true individualist against any form of collectivism."

"Sure, I guess," he shrugs. "Have I proven that I know something about philosophy?"

"Something," I chuckle.

"I'll be honest, I just saw a movie about him one time," he finally admits. "I do read books. Just not philosophy. But, if you tell anyone I read, I'm gonna have to kill you."

"Don't worry," I tell him. "Your secret is safe with me."

And just like that, he's not annoying anymore. I don't know what he is at this point. But I feel like we've crossed some line, and I'm not sure if whether this territory is safer or more dangerous than the previous one.

We talk a little more about each other, and surprisingly, he keeps changing the topic to me instead of him. To every question I ask him which revolves around him, he asks me two regarding myself. Again, I'm not sure how I feel about that. But I know that I loved his Kierkegaard response. Even if he did get all that from a movie. Must have been a good one.

He checks his watch, and I realize that an hour has flown by.

"I gotta run," he tells me, getting up. "I really had a nice time."

"Me, too," I reply, but I'm not allowing myself to think more of this than it was. Just two acquaintances having a coffee. That is where all this nonsense will end.

"Can I see you again?" He asks.

I've been hoping for this question, but it still comes as a surprise.

"I... I don't know," I shrug.

"I can read about Kierkegaard for next time," he winks at me. "If that's what it takes to have a drink with you again."

"Isn't that too much effort?" I wonder.

He leans down towards me, his lips so close to my ear that I can feel the softness of his warm breath. "I think you're worth it," he says, pulling away. "I'm also hoping that next time we meet, you'll tell me your name, mystery girl."

And with those words, he disappears out of the café, leaving me stunned, surprised and excited. The worst combination of the three.

Chapter Four

Gabriel

"So, how's school?" My father asks, sitting opposite me at a lunch table.

The food has already arrived. He's made sure of it. He probably has exactly one hour, maybe even less, before he's headed for his next meeting. Sometimes, I feel like that's all I am to him, just another meeting in his busy schedule, but I can't even blame him, because that is how things have always been. Just the two of us, with him constantly gone, and mom long dead. I wish he'd speak about her more often, but every time I start the conversation, I feel like even after fifteen years, it's still too difficult for him to talk about it, so I don't push it. Years keep passing us by, and all we do is talk about superficial things like school and girls.

"You know, fine," I tell him, digging my fork into the coq au vin, which he pronounced perfectly when he ordered it, while I with my years and years of learning French would barely be able to say something intelligible. He'd occasionally comment on it, but I felt like I always sucked with languages.

"Just fine?" He lifts his gaze, as he brings his wine glass to his lips.

He always first takes a quick whiff of the wine. He thinks no one notices it, but they do. Even I do. As a kid, I found it silly. Now, I understand. Some wines really smell like heaven in a glass. But you'd have to have a palate for it, to recognize it. Too many beers with the guys have almost killed mine, and that's OK.

Then, he takes just one small, tiniest sip, which he rolls about in his mouth. To the left first, then to the right, and only then does he swallow it, clicking his mouth softly, immediately inhaling afterwards. If he likes it, he gives a barely perceptible nod. If he hates it, then he'll surely let you know, and a new bottle will be immediately brought out. No one ever wants to offend William Price, the CEO of Emerald Price

Industries. Because if they do, one word from him and they'd be done. Gone. Totaled.

"Is everything to your liking, Mr. Price?" A waiter comes by, his shoulder slouching forward, as if he's constantly bowing in front of my father. I'm used to that. That was one of the other things I never understood as a child. But now I do.

"Yes, quite all right, thank you," my dad nods, doesn't even look at the guy. That's a cue for him to leave, and once again, we're alone.

"You know, I was thinking of taking two weeks off in July or August," he suddenly says. "Maybe we could travel to Spain or France, just the two of us, a father and son trip."

"Sure thing, dad," I nod, but I already know that's not going to happen.

It's like a dance we do every summer. He's been promising me this trip since I was fifteen. The first time he suggested it, I was more excited than I've ever been. Knowing him, we'd go to the best hotel, we'd eat the best food and we'd be treated like royalty, in Paris of all places. I was looking forward to it, I was even making little exes on my online calendar, waiting for the month he'd mentioned. When it finally arrived, he gave me some excuse about it being imperative for him to remain in NYC and sorting out some business matters that were urgent. He couldn't go. He was sorry. He'd make it up to me. I agreed. And that was how it went every single year from then on. He'd suggest it. I'd agree. Then the time came, and he could never get the time off. At some point, I stopped raising my hopes. It just wasn't worth it. Still, I understood that he was working for us, for him and for me, so we'd have everything we could ever need. Only sometimes, I needed him. I didn't need the money. I never told him that. I guess that truth was like his trip. The time just didn't come yet, and we were both waiting for it.

"Is there anything new going on?" He asks.

I appreciate the effort. I really do. But sometimes, like right now, I feel like our conversations have become forced. The closeness between us is almost completely gone. Mom was the one who kept reminding us that family is the most important thing in the world. She was the glue keeping us all together, and I guess that it was exactly because of her that dad spent more time at home. When she died, after a short but painful illness, he got lost in work. It was as if work was his only solace. He could focus on it and not think about anything else, not about his beautiful dead wife, or about his son who still needed him.

"No, nothing really," I reply. "Same old."

"Any girls?"

There were always girls. I never say that in that way, of course. But right now, I couldn't even say that. There were no girls at the moment. Only one. And, she hasn't even done anything to deserve my attention. She was just herself, and that alone was enough to wrap my focus. She's managed to do that with her clothes intact, with just smiling and even talking back to me. All ofAll that makes me want to see her again, even if it just to hear her say that we annoy each other too much and this could never work. Because it couldn't. We're too different. Yet, that's the best part.

"I take it that silence means there is someone?" Dad looks at me with his eyebrow raised, and I realize he's really curious about this. I have to admit, when he was with me, this one hour, he really focused on me. His phone wouldn't ring. I suppose he keeps it on silent. It's those little things that show me that despite everything, he still cares, only in his own special way.

"Well... I don't know..." I admit, raking my fingers through my hair, grinning stupidly.

"That's a good sign," he smiles widely.

He so rarely does it nowadays. He's always pleasant, but serious. I've witnessed him speak to some of his employees, even the higher ranked ones, and he's always polite, even when he's super upset. But a smile? That was mostly reserved for my mother. When she died, a part of him died with her as well, a part that I doubted would ever come back.

"Like I said, I honestly don't know what's going on there," I try to explain something I myself am not sure of. "There is someone, but we're not dating or anything yet."

"Why not?"

"We only met a week ago," I shrug. "Plus, I don't think I left a very good impression, but I did take her out to coffee."

"That's a good start."

"I think so, too."

"I know it's not my place to say anything," he suddenly starts, and the intimacy of his words somehow seems misplaced, as if he's not the right person who should be saying that. "But I would like to see grandkids before I die."

"Grandkids?" I frown. "Dad, I'm still in college. Don't you think you're getting a little ahead of yourself?"

"I won't live forever, Gabriel," he adds, whispering.

"I don't wanna talk about you dying, dad," I grimace. "This was supposed to be a nice, pleasant lunch, and now it's turned into planning your funeral."

"Well, now, we haven't gone that muchfar," he smiles again. "I'm merely reminding you that life won't go on forever. Mine won't. Neither will yours. You need to seize the moment. If you want something, you go get it. You be unapologetic about it. If it's meant to be yours, it will be yours. But you first have to make an effort to get it. Nothing will fall into your lap, while you sit, waiting and doing nothing. Remember that."

"I will, dad," I nod. That's also something he mentions often. I wonder if it he even knows that he's repetitive. But I say nothing.

"Let's have some dessert," he says. "I'm in the mood for some lava cake."

That was mom's favorite. They had their own special little French place, where they served the best lava cake in all of NYC.

"I'll have one, too," I smile back.

He lifts his hand, and the waiter appears immediately. Two lava cakes are ordered, and the waiter is gone as quickly as he's appeared taking away our empty plates.

"I don't want you to think I'm rushing you into anything," dad adds a little nervously. Every time our conversations become a little personal, he withdraws, becomes anxious and apologetic. Mom was always the one to handle tough conversations. She dealt with the first bully I had. She also dealt with my first fight, which was with that same bully, who left me alone after that. She also explained the birds and the bees, not him. Somehow, that was normal in our household. Mom was there for everything mental and psychological,psychological; dad was there for the material.

"I know," I nod. "It's OK. I know what you mean. I have no idea if this girl is the one. I don't even know what the one means. But she's the one that's intrigued me more than any other in a long time."

"It's important to distinguish girls who like you for you and girls who like you for your..." His voice trails off, and he doesn't really say it, but we both know what he means. Money. Name. Fame. The Price empire. Girls have heard of that, of course. I wonder if whether mystery girl has heard of it. Probably.

"I know," I repeat. "I'm taking things slowly with her. I want to see what she wants. And, who knows? Maybe we want the same thing."

He suddenly smiles at me, his wrinkles becoming more prominent. This smile makes me remember of mom, our trips together, late night pizza and movie watching, picnics in the backyard and star gazing. Things seemed so easy with mom around, so perfect. Without her, the world is incomplete. That is why I can't blame dad for becoming the way he is. He just didn't know how to handle losing her. He still doesn't know. He is still buried in his work because that is the only thing that provides any comfort. Perhaps my comfort was mindless sex. It was pretty comfortable, soothing even. But now, I don't want it any longer, and it's making me wonder why. I be bet Ashley is equally surprised by this turn of events.

"I'm happy to see the man you've grown up into," he suddenly tells me. "I know I haven't been there for you and look at you... you turned out so well, all on your own."

"I am who I am, because of mom and you," I remind him. "You've shaped me."

"I could have..."

But he isn't allowed to continue. Our lava cakes arrive, and the waiter places them in front of us. They smell divine. A small scoop of vanilla ice cream is placed right next to it. Mom never ate the ice cream. She always gave it to me. She said that her teeth didn't particularly enjoy the sensation of hot and cold together, and as a kid, I welcomed that, knowing that meant I'd get to eat her ice cream, too. Now I'd rather have it the other way around, her not having sensitive teeth and enjoy her ice cream.

I dig my spoon into the lava cake, and molten hot chocolate oozes from the very middle. Dad takes a bite, too. Satisfaction is etched on his face. I know he is overwhelmed by memories, too. We eat our cakes in silence, enjoying each other's company.

Chapter Five

Ava

"Oh, shit..." I whisper softly to myself when I lift my gaze and realize that I'm the only one left in the college library. All the little lamps are still on, but apart from ne, there is no one.

I always tend to do this, lose track of time when I do research for any paper. I've realized that I can focus much better here, in the soft, fragrant silence of this vast place, cozied up in between all these books. It soothes me somehow, in addition to boosting my inspiration. But sometimes I overdo it, and I stay way too late.

I check my phone. Getting hungry over here. Sylvia sent me a message. I almost forgot that we were inviting Rose and Beth from the room opposite our own, to order a pizza and watch a movie. It was supposed to be a girl's night, scheduled for pretty late, because we wanted to lock the doors and not open it for anyone.

Starting. I reply to Sylvia. Get the pizza.

OK. She replies, adding a little smiley to it.

I grab my notebooks and stuff them in my backpack. I take the two library books and walk over to the desk. Mrs. Wilkins is still there, staring at her computer screen, typing with both her index fingers. It takes her forever. The poor thing is almost eighty. She is months away from her retirement. I don't know why they decided to make her final days here a torture, by making her learn this new program for inputting all the books in it.

"Mrs. Wilkins?" I call out to her gently, but she still lifts her head, all startled.

"Oh, Ava, dear," she smiles. "It's you." She's looking at me from behind Coke bottle glasses, but no amount of squinting behind them would sharpen my image for her.

"I'm sorry, I didn't mean to scare you."

"It's quite all right, dearie," she is still smiling. "I just thought that I was the only one left in here. Then you pop up, out of nowhere."

"I lost track of time," I explain, placing the books on the counter that separates them.

"You always seem to," she reminds me.

I nod. "Well, I'd best return to my room."

"Stay safe, dearie," she says, as her eyes glance at me, but I'm not even sure she sees me properly.

"I will," I wave turning around and heading for the exit.

I wonder why she advised me to stay safe. Maybe because it's dark? It's probably because she belongs to another time, a time when good girls were home by night fall, so nothing bad could happen to them.

Suddenly, as if on cue, my mind starts listing all the things that could happen to good girls as they walk home alone at night. I remember all the horror movies I've seen, all the books real and invented I've read about horrible things happening to girls and—

No. I immediately stop myself from continuing that list. Nothing is happening on campus grounds. That is the safest place around. The whole place is lit up. There are guards in every building. All I have to do, if I get scared, is walk a bit more quickly and I'll be in my dorm in less than fifteen minutes.

Still, that doesn't help my sudden sense of anxiety. I know Mrs. Wilkins meant well, but all she managed to do was plant a seed of fear inside of me, which knowing me, will keep on growing until I slam the door of my dorm room from the inside. Damn this susceptible mind of mine.

I hasten my step, sliding my thumb under the straps of my backpack which hangs on my back. My eyes keep darting left and right. Every shadow is a monster, ever flicker of a light is a possible threat.

I keep reminding myself that this is silly. I'm being ridiculous. Nothing will happen. What could happen here? Still, I keep walking faster and faster, and at one point I'm almost running.

Then, suddenly, I hear it. The sound of a cracked branch somewhere right behind me. I turn around immediately, but I don't stop moving. Now, I'm walking backwards, not stopping, my heart beating in my heels, keeping me going, keeping me afloat. I can't stop. Some urge deep down keeps telling me that something terrible might happen if I stop.

So, I don't. I keep moving, and that sensation of fear is getting stronger by the moment, although I see nothing before me and nothing behind me. It was probably just a stupid squirrel or something, I try to calm myself down but the darkness around me is overpowering.

I turn around and walk even more quickly. I'm almost running now.

"Ava…"

Someone whispers my name loudly enough for me to hear it. This time, I stop. I turn around again, my fingers curling up into fists. I have a pencil in my backpack I could use for self-defense if I need to, but I'd have to find it first, and I don't want to take my eyes off my surroundings even for a single second. What if someone jumps out at me and I'm not ready?

I stare at the darkness around me. The lamp posts are illuminating the grounds, but there are still so many shadows, and that is where my brain starts to play tricks on me. All my childhood fears come to the surface, all the monsters under the bed and from the closet, all the scary stories and all the nightmares.

I start running now, my sneakers flying off the ground, and relief washes over me as I see the outlines of my dorm building. I run as fast as I can, almost slamming against the glass door, which I quickly push open then close behind me, still breathing heavily. Only then do I realize that the guard is eyeing me weirdly.

"Is everything OK?" He asks, tilting his head a little as he's watching me, probably trying to figure out if I'm drunk or high.

"Yeah, just..." I start, swallowing heavily, turning around, and looking through the glass door. I see nothing. The night is peaceful as always around here. "Nothing." I shake my head dismissively.

"Are you sure?" He wonders. "You don't look like it's nothing."

"I'm OK, really," I reply much calmer this time. "Mrs. Wilkins, the librarian, told me to stay safe, and I guess my mind made it into a big deal, almost thinking that someone was following me, but I guess it's all in my mind."

From the look on his face, I can tell that he's not all that certain. "You know what they say about gut feelings, Miss."

"No need to call me, Miss.," I smile at the guy who is maybe five years older than me. "I'm Ava."

"Clayton," he introduces himself. He's heavily built, although he's not overweight. The night guard uniform suits him perfectly, as he has that dose of authority about him. "But I did mean that thing about the gut feeling."

"I know," I nod. "I'm sure it was nothing."

I decide not to mention hearing someone whisper my name. Perhaps that never really happened. The mind is a powerful tool. It can make you see and hear things that aren't really there. I don't want to appear crazy.

"I could go outside and check the premises, if that would make you feel safer," he suggests.

"Oh, I couldn't ask you to do that," I say, although a part of me doesn't think it's a bad idea. At least, I'll sleep more soundly, assure assured that it really was all in my mind.

"Nonsense," he says, immediately getting up. "That's my job. It's why I'm here." He opens a drawer and takes out a flashlight, turning it on and flashing it through the glass door and into the distance. "I'll just go have a little stroll, just to see everything is peaceful."

"Well... OK," I nod, feeling strangely appeased by this. "I really appreciate it."

"That's fine," he smiles. His short curly hair is pointing in all directions, throwing a funny shadow on the floor. "You just go on to your room. I'll make sure nothing's out there. Like you said, I'm also sure it's nothing, but it doesn't hurt to be extra safe these days."

"You're right," I confirm. "Thanks again, Clayton."

"You're welcome, Ava," he replies, pronouncing my name somehow importantly, as if he couldn't wait to say it again.

"Good night," I tell him, as I disappear into the hallway that leads up the stairs to the first floor, where my room is.

I reach my room quickly, opening it immediately, almost barging in.

"Hey," I hear Sylva frown at me. "Where's the fire?"

I quickly close the door, and for some reason, I rest against themit, as if I'm half-expecting someone to be following me and try to come inside.

"Are you OK?" Sylvia asks, realizing that this isn't the time for jokes.

"Yeah," I nod, with a deep inhale. "Just... had the weirdest feeling of someone following me on the way back from the library."

"Following you?"

Sylvia always takes these things very seriously, because her best friend was assaulted a few years ago, and luckily, the girl had mace on her, so the guy got a decent dose of it, allowing her to escape unharmed. They never caught the guy, though. I can't even imagine what that must feel like, to know that there was someone out there who wanted to hurt you, who planned on doing it, and who was foiled just because you were clever enough to seize your chance, spray him and run away. I wonder if that girl still fears going out alone in the dark. I shudder at the thought.

"I mean, I didn't see anyone, but I had such a strong feeling," I explain, finally moving away from the door. "I think I even heard someone whisper my name, but now I'm wondering if it wasn't only the wind."

"Yeah, the wind speaks English, and it knows your name," Sylvia knits her eyebrows at me. "Come on, Ava."

"OK, then it probably was someone following me and trying to freak me out. And they did a very good job of it," I conclude. "Clayton said he'd go check it out."

"Clayton?"

"The new night guard?" I say. "I haven't seen him before, but he was nice enough to introduce himself and even go check out the premises."

"Oh, my," Sylvia winks at me, playfully. "We got a knight in shining night guard armor here."

"Stop it," I chuckle. "He seems like a very nice guy."

"I'm sure he is," she shrugs defensively. "And he probably expects something nice in return."

"Well, he won't begettingbe getting anything in return," I reply. "Except maybe a thank you coffee or something brought to his desk. That should be enough."

"Because you like someone else," Sylva suddenly points at me. "You like the pretty boy, don't you?"

"I do not," I frown. "We just had a coffee yesterday and it's not like–
"

"Wait... you what??"

Only then do I realize that I haven't told her about the book, the bet and the coffee. I've been meaning to, but I knew this would happen. She'd think I'm falling for him, and I'm not. I'm really not.

"Like I said, it was just a coffee," I shrug. "No big deal."

I'm not really sure who I'm lying to here, her or myself. But I still stick to what I said.

"OK, if you say so," she nods, but I can tell that she doesn't believe a single thing I've told her. I decide to let it go.

"Are the girls ready?" I ask, looking about. I see the pizza is already here.

"I was waiting for you to come. I'll send Beth a message to come over."

"Great," I smile. "I need a distraction."

"Seems like you've had enough distraction this week, girl," she says sympathetically this time.

"You're right. Then, a peaceful evening with the girls is exactly what the doctor ordered."

"You know it," she smiles, grabbing her phone to send a message.

I know it's silly, but I still feel that fear in the back of my mind. Was it really just the wind, or was someone calling out to me from the shadows?

Chapter Six

Gabriel

"I didn't think you'd come," I tell her, as we're sitting in a restaurant this time, not a café.

"I couldn't say no," she replies. "You took my book with you."

"Ah, yes," I chuckle, lifting my wine glass to her. I won't be driving back anyway, so I figured a nice glass of wine would be a welcome change from the beer I usually have. "I had to be sure you'd come."

"So, you thought sticky fingers would help you?" She asks, but I can see that she is amused.

"Your attention was focused elsewhere," I explain. "It was easy to just pick it up and take it with me."

I watch as she blushes slightly, her cheeks taking on a sweetly innocent pinkish hue. I don't remember the last time I've seen a girl blush. It suits her perfectly. Everything about her is perfectly measured, from the depth of her curls to the few stray freckles that cover the tip of her nose and the outer edge of her cheeks like a miniature explosion of stars.

"Well, I do think resourcefulness should be rewarded," she tells me, and I know that she wants to be here as much as I do.

It's crazy. This whole thing is totally insane, and yet I can't seem to pull away from this magnetic field that is around her. I'm drawn to her more than I've ever been drawn to a girl, and I can't tell if it's just because she's playing hard to get or because she is just herself. Whatever the answer to that question is, I know I have to find out.

"Now, that's something we can both agree on," I smile watching her take the glass and raise it to me.

At that moment, the waiter comes, bringing the food. "The salmon for the lady, and the beef for the gentleman," he announces.

"Thank you," she says first, and I echo her words.

"Enjoy your meal," he bows quickly. "And, may I say, you two seem like such a compatible couple."

"Oh, no," she immediately points at me, shaking her head. "He's not my... I mean, we're not a couple."

A part of me doesn't like it that she jumped so quickly to express her status as still single, but then again, of course she's not lying. Then why wasn't I indifferent to her comment? This evening just keeps getting weirder and weirder.

"I'm sorry," the waiter lifts his hands in a stance of mock surrender. "It is I who have crossed the line, making that comment. It's just that I have made it a daily goal to compliment one stranger. Sometimes Something of a personal improvement goal as well."

"That's so sweet," she smiles. "We do appreciate the comment, though."

She said we. That makes me feel a little better. She didn't used the singular form only for herself.

"Yeah, man," I nod, not wanting to make the guy feel embarrassed because although it was weird to just throw it out there like that, it still came from a good place. He didn't mean it to sound weird. It was the opposite actually. He sounds like a good guy who's just a bit awkward. "It's totally fine. No need to apologize."

"Thank you both," the waiter says apologetically. "I'll allow you to enjoy your meal. I apologize again."

He disappears as quickly as he's appeared, and both Ava and I catch each other's eye, suppressing a bout of laughter.

"Well, that was a bit awkward," I whisper, leaning across the table.

"I still think it was sweet," she replies. "Not everyone is born to be in the spotlight like you, you know. Some people are introverts, like me. We find it pretty awkward to talk to other people, especially if we don't know them."

"You don't seem to have any trouble talking to me," I notice, glad for the realization.

"You annoyed me," she tells me, with a grin.

"Annoyed? As in past tense?" I tease.

"Don't make me turn it back to the present tense," she threatens jokingly, and we both laugh.

It's an effortless laughter. I don't find myself talking bullshit as usual. Not that any of the girls before had any idea what I was talking about. They would laugh and giggle anyway. That does wonders for your ego, but eventually, it starts to get old. Maybe that was the reason I could never see myself with Ashley. She's gorgeous, but there's something missing, something to make us click somehow. I never felt that with her, while the message is loud and clear with Ava.

We start eating, and she turns silent. She lifts her gaze to me occasionally, but we mostly finish our meal in silence. Immediately upon finishing, the waiter comes again.

"Was everything to your liking?"

"Yes, it was delicious," she answers first. Then, she glances over at me. "Are we having dessert?"

I try not to seem surprised, although I am. The girls I hang out with wouldn't be caught dead eating dessert. They're always on this diet or that diet, which doesn't allow desserts or cheat days. And eating dessert alone is no fun. Desserts are meant to be eaten in company.

"Absolutely," I nod. "What are you in the mood for?"

"I was thinking maybe lava cake?" She wonders and I suppress a sudden cough. My saliva slides down the wrong way, and I immediately try to clear it up, coughing loudly this time.

"Are you OK?" She asks. "Do you want some water?"

I lift my hand to her, shaking my head, handling the last bouts of coughing. When I can finally inhale again, I speak. "I'm fine. It's just that I was thinking of ordering the same thing."

I know what it sounds like, I'm doing this on purpose, and I want her to think that we have so much in common. But it's not on purpose at all. Lava cakes are my favorite dessert. They remind me of my mother, my childhood. Only I don't want to share that with her yet. It's too early for such personal confessions. This is only our second date, and I don't want to scare her off. I surprise even myself when my wishes finally make themselves known. I want her to stick around for a while. A long while.

"In that case, two lava cakes, please," she tells the waiter, and this time, he makes no weird comments. He just nods, then leaves and shortly returns with two beautifully served desserts. The smell brings back memories, which I'd rather not think about now. They always put me in some melancholic mood, and that's not where I want to be right now. I want to be here, present in the moment, with her.

I watch as she takes a small spoon and digs into the dessert. There is no ice cream served next to the small cup. I don't say anything. It doesn't matter. The look of satisfaction on her face assures me that she's happy with what she's received, and that's all that matters.

We finish out dessert, and I call the waiter to pay.

"Cash or card?"

"Card," I nod.

He leaves again, and I notice she's looking at me. "I want to pay for my own half," she tells me.

I smile. "Why?"

"Because that's only fair."

"Why?" I repeat equally amused. "I was under the impression that the one who invites is the one who treats. You treated me to the coffee, and I'm treating you to the dinner. Doesn't that seem fair to you?"

She obviously wasn't expecting me to say this. I must say, I also wasn't expecting her to pay for her share of the meal. Girls usually have no problem being treated to more than just a dinner. I'm usually a generous guy, but even I have limits. With Ava, it seems that she is the one setting those limits for me.

"I guess," she finally agrees.

"You like when things are fair, don't you?"

"Well…" she seems surprised by my question. "Doesn't everyone?"

"I guess," I nod, repeating her own phrase from a moment ago. "But, sometimes, things are fair or unfair in someone else's favor. Like, for example, paying for this dinner. Why wouldn't you just let me pay for it, because we're having a nice time, and I enjoy you being here, as my guest and I feel good about treating you? What's so wrong with that?"

"You mean that patriarchal constituency?" She frowns.

"Just because I paid for your meal doesn't make you my inferior, if that's what you're afraid of happening here," I explain, realizing what she wants to do. She doesn't want to make herself appear to be like all the other girls. She would never say it out loud, of course, but I see no other explanation for this.

"Of course, it doesn't," she confirms. "I just don't want to feel like I owe you something just because you paid for the dinner."

"Then, don't," I smile. "Just enjoy the meal and say thank you, it's my treat next time."

"What if I don't want there to be a next time?" She asks, and I feel that bout of coughing oncoming, but I manage to keep it under control. I have to admit, I didn't see this one coming. I thought we were having a great time. I've been trying to find a way to ask her out again, but she's making it increasingly more difficult, and me, the stupid idiot just want it more. The more she pulls away, the more I reach out. How stupid can I be?

"That is your decision, and I will of course, honor it," I say as politely as I can. I even mean it. "But if you do change your mind about it, I'll be happy to take you out again, and have you pay for everything."

She smiles. The waiter comes and interrupts our conversation, putting the bill on the table right between us. I give her a moment, but she doesn't reach for it. So, I take it, and pay it without a word. Once the waiter is gone, I smile back at her.

"There is nothing wrong with being treated to little things," I shrug. "Especially if it's done by someone who cares about you."

I wish I'd bitten mt tongue before saying that, but it's too late. She's heard it. I've heard it, too. I said someone who cares about you.

"You care about me?" She wonders, with a flicker of a smile gracing those luscious, full lips.

The moment of truth. I could just play it off as a joke, a mere play on words. I could say I meant it as a generic statement about anyone, not particularly us. But I don't do any of that.

"I think so," I admit.

Fuck it. I'm so tired of playing games and constantly keeping a mask on. I wonder what will happen if I'm just honest, without the constant need to impress others and make them think I'm the best thing since sliced bread.

"You don't even know me," she urges, but the tone of her voice is warm, welcoming. She is curious, not disbelieving.

"That's why I'm here," I explain. "That's why I kept asking you out, determined to ask more times than you say no. Because I want to get to know you."

There is a pregnant pause in the air, filled with so much possibility. I want to invite her over to my place, but I don't want her to think I'm just after one thing. Because I'm not. I want that, but I also want to wake up next to her, and continue this conversation, and keep having it for a long time.

"I don't know if you want to get to know me, but– "

"You wanna get outta here?" She asks, and that mischievous grin tugs at my very insides, lighting up a flame.

"I thought you'd never ask," I grin back.

Chapter Seven

Ava

His place is definitely not what I expected, and I guess that much is obvious from the look on my face. There are paintings on the wall, a soft palette of earthy colors which feels soothing on the eyes. The whole living room is minimalistic, but with all the important elements still present, like the huge screen tv screen hanging off the wall right opposite the sofa.

"You expected the red-light district?" He chuckles, behind me, bringing me another glass of wine in what appear to be a thin, delicate wine glass.

""Are you trying to get me drunk?" I ask, not refraining from the wine he's just brought over.

"I'm that transparent, huh?" He winks at me, and I'm not sure if it's the wine or just me getting unhinged, but I feel something inside of me melt.

I can see the way he's looking at me, undressing me with his eyes. I can see it, because I'm doing the same. This wine has helped me admit it to myself, that I do find him incredibly hot, and every bit of me wants to know what it feels like to have him touch me, to make me melt even more than this. We're two consenting adults, after all. There is no need to hold back. I just have to remind myself not to expect too much from him. Just this one night of mind-blowing sex, hopefully, and we'll both grow tired of each other quickly enough.

He sits next to me on the sofa. I remind myself not to get attached to him. This is just temporary. He smiles at me, and all that effort feels as if it's gone to waste.

"I don't want you to think that just because we're here that we need to do anything," he suddenly says, just as I'm expecting him to kiss me.

I'm slightly disappointed, but even more surprised at his sudden show or chivalry. I nod.

"That's nice of you," I reply, biting my tongue so as not to tell him that it's completely unnecessary and I know why I'm here. I'm here for the same reason he is. To have fun and get him out of my system.

Throughout our dinner, I could feel the heartbeat of desire palpitating underneath every word I said to him. He must know that I want it as much as he does.

He leans closer to me, and our fingers intertwine. The next thing I know, my arms fly around his neck. It is me who's pressing my lips to his, getting closer, drawn by his raw animalistic magnetism. His lips are softer than I could have imagined them. Pliant. They are as hungry as mine are. He tastes like wine, and I want to drink more of it from his lips.

A tidal wave of desire washes over me. I'm unable to control myself. I want him to take me, to take all of me. Still kissing him with a breath that feels like the last breath I would ever take, my mind and heart are at war with each other. A desperation has awoken inside of me as sharp as the blade of a sword. It is slicing right through me, ridding me of the shackles I once carried.

I'm not myself tonight. It might be the wine, but it might be my true self, emerging. The play of his tongue with my own is enough to drive me insane. I cup his face with my hands, biting his lower lip. He groans against me, the tremor waking us both.

His lips travel to the corner of mine, then down my chin and my jaw. I hear him inhale my scent, and an explosion of wetness hits me between my thighs. He keeps dragging his mouth down my neck, his tongue licking my skin which has been sensitized to the brim.

His hands are on the curves of my waist, pulling me closer to him. I want him to tear these clothes off ofoff me, but he takes it slow. Painfully slow. I press my hands to his chest, feeling his rock-hard muscles. He tries to find the zipper to my dress but is unable to.

"How do you take this darn thing off?" He chuckles, his warm breath setting me on fire.

I unzip it right underneath my armpit, and I slide out of it. The strap of my bra falls down to my elbows, as he trails his fingers down my neck, chest, stopping right before he removes the part of my bra which is hiding my nipples.

"We can still stop," he tells me, breathless. "I don't want you to think that the only reason I brought you here was to– "

"Shhh," I press my finger to his lips. I don't want him to be nice. I want him to be exactly the opposite. I want him to be an animal, a beast, because I feel like I'm going to die unless he's inside of me in the next five minutes.

As if on cue, his fingers skillfully expose my breasts, and his lips immediately dive down. The wetness of his mouth and his tongue is enough to send me over the edge. I moan loudly, as he keeps playing with my perked upperked-up nipples. I reach for his pants, trying to unbutton them. I feel his hard cock, straining against the fabric of his jeans. Heat laces through me. I'm delirious, needy, longing, all because of him.

"Fuck..." He groans, as I grab a handful of his cock through his jeans.

"Take them off," I whisper, both of us completely losing any leftover ability to think.

He jumps up, and quickly wiggles out of his jeans and t-shirt. Then, he drops down to his knees before me, spreading my legs apart.

"I'd like nothing better than to fuck your brains right now," he tells me mischievously, "but, patience is a virtue."

Before I can say anything, he sucks a nipple into his month, tugging at it with his teeth. I moan again, digging my fingers into his hair. His tongue keeps licking at my tender skin, as he listens to my sounds of desire.

He pulls away, kissing down my stomach, lingering on my bellybutton. His hands slide underneath my butt, pulling down the delicate lacey panties I chose just for the occasion. I'd be lying if I said I wasn't planning on showing them off.

My panties fly across the room, as he kisses down to my thighs, making sure I keep my legs open, revealing myself to him. Crazy with desire just like I am, he flicks his tongue over my clit. My hips immediately buckle in response, as he lifts my butt with his hands a little, getting me closer to his lips.

"Oh... my... God..." I bite my lower lip, as he runs his tongue right between the wet folds, sucking on them, biting them softly, only to slide inside again and again. I grab a handful of his hair, tugging at it, following his rhythm. My hips are thrusting back at him, as he drives deeper into me, refusing to slow down his pace. He brought me to the brink too quickly, and all I can do is let go, as he sucks on my clit slowly, teasingly, until my entire body quivers, and right before I implode, he slides a finger into me, only intensifying the sensation.

My insides contract, and I feel I am transformed into liquid heat, as he slides his finger into me again and again, pressing his lips to my palpitating clit, and all I can do is moan with pleasure.

When my body calms down a little, he withdraws, but not before he kisses the inside of both my thighs.

""I take it you're pleased?" He asks tantalizingly, pressing his lips to my naked hip bone. I just chuckle, released releasing the tight grip I had on his hair, and he kisses his way up my stomach, all the way up to my exposed breasts. He sucks one of my nipples in, only to bite teasingly, then blows on it, making it even harder than it was a moment ago.

"I want more," I dare to tell him surprising even myself with this animal who's surfaced, completely shadowing the Ava everyone knows. I cup his face, pulling him closer to me, so that our eyes are staring into each other now. Neither of us refrains from this stare of sheer intimacy. Instead, we welcome it.

"Whatever the lady desires," he replies, his voice almost a whisper, as he presses his lips to mine again, devouring me. I taste myself on his tongue, a seductive musk mixed with the wine we both just had. Yet, I don't pull away. Everything about tonight is carnal and overpowering, and I can't refuse him anything.

I lower my hand down, pulling his boxer shorts down enough to release his raging cock. I guide it to my entrance, both of us throbbing with need. He can feel my wetness, my hot center, and all I want is to feel him inside of me. But suddenly, he gets up and runs to the other room. He returns a few moments later, with a torn condom wrapper, which he's already putting on. I smile. He returns to the same position, and as if he can read my mind, he thrusts inside of me.

I close my eyes, throwing my head back on the sofa, biting my lower lip. It's too much. He's thick and long, filling me to the brim. He made me cum once, and I doubted I'd be able to do it again tonight. My body needs to rest. It needs to recharge. But it's like it's not my body at all. It's a body with a mind of its own, and all it wants is to get fucked from here to infinity. Every part of me feels like he just bathed me in fire. I'm tingling. I'm brimming. I'm on the brink or exploding, imploding, melting completely in his arms, as his cock slides in and out of me effortlessly, bringing a new tidal wave of sensation with each thrust.

We're both breathless. I feel him palpitating and huge inside of me. It's better than anything I could have imagined. His thrusts suddenly become deeper, harder, and I grind myself against him shamelessly, as if clutching to my dear life. I'm feverish, as I push myself to wait just a few moments longer, as pleasure builds up inside of me.

Frantic, he slams his mouth against mine, our bodies pounding in unison, locked in together for eternity. We both cum at the same time, ecstasy turning my vision black, so I close my eyes, but even like that, I see thousands and thousands of little stars, exploding one at a time. His kisses suddenly become gentler, and a moment later, he slides out of me.

He sits on the sofa, wrapping his arms around me, pulling me closer to him in a cuddle. I smile, not expecting this. I glance at the floor, at my clothes. As soon as this unexpected outburst of tenderness ends, I'm getting dressed and going back home.

He doesn't say anything, and I notice that his eyes are closed, so I try to gently move away from him, but he notices immediately.

"Yeah, good idea," he says, seeing me get up. "Let's go to bed."

"I'm not going to bed," I correct him. "I'm going home."

I adjust my bra straps, then slide into my panties, still feeling a bit wet, but not unpleasantly so.

"Why?" He suddenly jumps up and faces me. "Did I do something wrong?"

"No," I chuckle. "You did everything right, even more than right."

"Then, why don't you spend the night here?"

"No," I shake my head.

Everything inside of me is telling me to stay. I'm tired. I want to sleep. I can just go back home tomorrow morning. But that's not the real reason why I don't want to do this. If I spend the night, I'll have to accept things which I'm still not ready to accept. So, it's safest for me to just go now.

I'm fully dressed now, and he's still looking at me. I approach him, cupping his cheeks with my palms, and pressing my lips to his.

"That was great, but we both knew that's all it was," I remind him.

"No," he shakes his head. "I... that's not what I wanted I wasn't looking for just a fuck."

"What did you want then?"

Careful. My mind is urging me to be careful, but my hopes have flared despite all common sense. Guys like him are not to be trusted. I know this. I've seen this with my own eyes. Girls are just checks in his little black book, which he probably discusses with his friends. I want to think the worst of him, but I can't. That little voice inside of me keeps reminding me not to stereotype everyone, not to put them all in the same basket, because there is an exception to every rule. Every fiber in my being is hoping that Gabriel Price is the exception to this rule.

"I have girls lining up for a one nightone-night stand with me," he frowns. "I admit that I was sleeping around before. Everyone knows this. Not like I ever tried to keep it a secret. But that's not what I want. Not anymore."

I swallow heavily. He's telling me the truth. He's never tried to hide or lie about who he was. Of course, he wouldn't be able to because everyone knows him, but still. If he keeps talking this way, I'll be in deep trouble. I need to keep him at a distance, even if I do agree to seeing him again.

"We can meet up again, but I still won't spend the night."

"Why not?"

Because then I'll have to admit that I'm in love with him, that I'm as stupid as all those other bimbos who run after popular guys, waiting and hoping for a single smile or a slap on the butt only to giggle in appreciation. That's not who I am, and yet, I have fallen for the same type. Luckily, I don't say this out loud.

"Because I have plans with Sylvia for early in the morning," I lie, blushing immediately.

"How early?" He asks. "I'll take you back to campus."

"No, why would you? It's Sunday. You should sleep in, rest, do whatever you do on a Sunday, and we'll just talk over the week."

I can tell he wants to convince me to stay, but I can't. I can't let him convince me. So, I grab my purse and I'm already by the door.

"I can drive you back," he offers.

"We both had drinks," I remind him. "I'll just call a cab. Don't worry."

"Text me when you get home?" He urges, following me to the door. "No, actually, wait." He returns to put on his clothes and comes back again. "I'm going to wait for the cab with you."

"You don't have to do that."

"If you're not staying the night, that's the least I can do."

I nod, realizing that he won't be taking no for an answer. He walks me down two flights of stairs and does as he vowed. He hugs me and kisses me tenderly the moment we see my cab arrive. I wave at him, feeling a little awkward, and don't turn around to see whether he's still there once in the car. Luckily, the cab driver is a quiet guy, so I don't have to talk when I'm not really in the mood for it.

I close my eyes, allowing the memories to flood me. I can't help but smile. I didn't spend the night, but it seems that what I feared most has already happened.

Chapter Eight

Gabriel

So, this is what walking on cloud nine feels like.

Fuck, I feel like a schoolboy who just kissed his crush and then got to hold her hand in front of everyone, proving that she was his sweetheart now. Only, we did so much more than kissing. My whole body still tenses at the very thought of her name, and I have no idea how I'll go through an entire afternoon of lectures, focusing on numbers and theories. It'll be tough.

I check my watch as I'm rushing through the campus ground. A part of me is looking around, hoping I'll stumble onto her. It's been only a day, you moron. That sensible voice inside of me tries to instill some reason in me, as always, but I'm too deep already. Usually, it's me who's the one looking about for the exact opposite reason. I'm trying to avoid girls I slept with, because they always want to stop, chat, invite me over again, in hopes that something more will develop eventually. It never does and I always make sure to be clear about this.

Speaking of which… I see a familiar face head straight for me across the manicured lawn in between the two main buildings. Just a moment earlier, I could have looked away and headed in the other direction. But I've already noticed her. Her face lit up the moment our eyes met. Don't be a jackass, that voice says. Despite what everyone thinks, I'm not an asshole. I try to do right by the girls whose hearts I might have broken.

"Hey, Gabriel," Ashley chirps the moment she comes within a hearing distance of me. I lift my hand to greet her.

She stops, so I do the same. It feels rude to just walk past her if she's already stopped. She steps on her toes, the way she usually did, and kisses me on the cheek. I notice she's wearing bright pink lipstick, and I instinctively wipe my cheek. It's not a color I particularly like, on girls or on myself.

"Don't worry," she tells me with a mischievous wink. "There is no trace."

"That's OK," I smile a little awkwardly.

When we're in a group, it feels fine talking to her. But when it's just the two of us, I know she'll steer the conversation in the direction I've been actively trying to avoid. Then again, maybe stating clearly again how things are and what not to expect might be beneficial for us both.

"How have you been?" She asks. "Haven't seen you at the Cappa Delta house on Saturday."

The party. I totally forgot about it. I was actually on a date with Ava that very evening. The party never even crossed my mind. So, that must be why Brandon's been calling all day yesterday, but when I tried to call him back in the evening, he didn't pick up. I figured he was busy with some chick or something. Now I might think he's upset I missed it. He was planning it for weeks, and even said he'd get that famous DJ that's all the rage right now. Shit. I guess you could say I'm not a very good friend right now, but I know once I explain to him what happened, he'll understand. We always do.

"Yeah," I rake my fingers through my hair, "I just... had somewhere else to be."

"Somewhere more important than us?"

"Us?" I frown. Is she referring to the two of us, the non-existent couple or our group of friends?

"Your friends?" She explains, with a save.

"Oh," I smile. "Well, you know I like spending time with you guys, but– "

"What's her name?" She interrupts me. I look at her, and notice she's not upset. I mean, why should she be? Not like we're together and I'm cheating on her. She's not upset, but I still sense a dose of something I don't like, something she shouldn't be feeling as just a friend.

My first response is to say whose name, but I decide against it. Why should I hide the fact I was on a date? I've been trying to protect her feelings and explain nicely that nothing will ever develop between us, what happened happened, and that was that. But she's pushing it and if she wants to hear it, so be it.

"Her name isn't important to anyone but me," I say, finally deciding that I won't be exposing Ava to Ashley's potentially rude comments.

"So, there is someone," she muses more to herself than to me.

"You just asked me that," I frown.

"True, I did. I was just hoping you'd say you were home alone, but what are the odds of that happening, right?"

This time, her comment is more venomous, much less friendly. So, I become the same. I didn't want to, but sometimes, being nice only prolongs the torture and people believe they can make you change your mind just because your no is polite and doesn't sound intimidating enough.

"You knew me from day one, Ash," I give her an indifferent half-shrug, because my conscience is clean. I've never lied to her, or any other girl I hooked up with. I pride myself on always telling the other side what they can and can't expect from me. "I told you what this is." I gesture at the two of us with my hand. "You can't say I lied to you or led you on."

"No, I can't," she admits, but she still sounds antagonistic. "But you can't blame a girl for falling in love."

"See, that's exactly what I advised you not to do," I remind her, trying not to sound annoyed, because I'm not. "Now we're in this awkward situation, and maybe it's not a good idea for us to hang out anymore, even with the others."

"You can't push me away like that."

She stands closer to me. She a little spitfire, even in bed. But I've always known that is the only place where I wanted her, and I made that perfectly clear.

"I'm not trying to push you away from me," I sigh, realizing that I might be in deep shit here. "I'm just suggesting that it might be a good idea for us not to see each other until you sort out your feelings."

"I will find out who she is," she tells me, as if she hasn't heard a single thing I've said. Her tone is menacing, as if she wants to threaten me with something, only I'm not sure with what exactly.

"And do what?" I feel like she is too close now, invading my personal space. Her eyebrows are lowered, and her jutting chin is pointed straight at me as she is lifting her eyes to meet mine. She's daring me to do something, to say something, but I don't react. That's what puts her off balance, not evoking any kind of a reaction.

"Are you scared I'll hurt your little kitten?" She asks, mockingly. I can hear her rapid breathing. Again, she's trying to get a rise out of me. I can't let her.

"Hurt?" I frown. "What the hell are you talking about, Ashley? Get a grip."

I sound like we're having a completely irrelevant conversation and it pisses her off even more.

"I just want you to take this as a promise, Gabriel," she gives me a tightlipped smile. "I will not back down. I will not stop seeing you just because you say so. You have a little girlfriend? That's fine. I'm sure you'll grow bored of her even faster than you grew bored of me. But then, I'll be waiting for you. When no one else wants you anymore, I'll be there. You'll realize how important I am to you, and you will come back to me in the end. I know all I have to do is stay patient. You'll find your way back to me..."

At this moment, I'm wondering if whether she's batshit crazy or something. Her flared nostrils and puffed chest show me that she's not kidding. This isn't a joke. She's seriously telling me that she won't leave me alone, like a dog marking its territory, she's trying to assure me that I belong to her, and she belongs to me. I never said any such thing, and I don't plan on saying it now.

"I've been nice all this time, Ash," I still try to speak to her, one friend to another, because I don't want her to get hurt in any way. But if she's threatening me or anyone dear to me, then she's got another thing coming. "I do care about you. You're a good friend. Don't make me regret thinking that."

"Oh, come on," she suddenly smacks my shoulder with her fist. "You don't think I'd start a catfight over you, do you?" She chuckles. "I mean, I'd win anyway. But I don't want to hurt anyone else either, even though she deserves it for stealing you away from me."

"No one stole me from you," I shake my head incredulously at her. At this point, I feel like I'm having a conversation with myself, and she's having one with herself, while our conversations interlap only in certain points.

"She did," she corrected me. "Otherwise, we'd still be hooking up, and you'd realize that we were meant to be together. But it's something you need to realize as well. I can't convince you of that."

"OK then..." I'm relieved that it seems we could bring this madness to an end, although still not totally persuaded. "I'm glad we're in agreement."

"But that doesn't mean I won't find out who she is. And I will tell her that what we have is more than what you two would ever have."

"What?" My eyes narrow at her, seeing we're back to square one.

"Once I tell her that I love you more than anyone could possibly love you, she will understand. A woman understands another woman in love. I know you've lost your way a little, but it's alright. I'll get you back. Don't worry..."

And with those words, she props herself up on her tiptoes once more, giving me a peck on the other cheek, then walks around me and leaves me standing there, completely stunned at what's just happened.

I try not to think about it too much, and just make a mental note to avoid her from now on, at least until she sorts this out with herself.

Suddenly, my phone rings, and I immediately pick up.

"You alive, man, or what?" Brandon shouts from the other side.

"Yeah," I nod. "I'm good. Sorry I bailed on Saturday."

"You had a good reason?"

"The best," I grin.

"In that case, bros are bros. We're good.'

"Thanks, man," I reply. "How was the party?"

I head for the main building to the left, still on the phone.

"We rocked the house," he tells me. "We had some serious honeys this time. You really missed out."

"I don't think so," I shake my head more to myself than to him.

"By the way, Ashley was looking for you all night," he adds. "You guys together or something?"

"No," I assure him. "We hooked up a few more times these past few months, but I've always been clear about my intentions with her."

"Yeah, maybe not clear enough."

"Fuck," I sigh. "I just stumbled onto her on the way to class. She kept saying stuff that she's in love with me and that she'll wait for me no matter how much time I need..."

"Sounds like she's really digging you."

"I'm afraid it's more than that. Sounds like she's obsessed with me."

"I wish she was obsessed with me, man," Brandon laughs loudly.

I smile, although I don't really feel like smiling. "She's all yours."

"Yeah, that doesn't work like that."

"Yeah," I nod. "You wanna come over tonight? We can order pizza and play some Xbox?"

"Sure," he agrees. "I can be there around eight."

"Sounds like a plan," I confirm. "See ya then."

I hang up the phone, my mind still focused on the incident with Ashley. She's always been... passionate. I guess that could be the right term for it. Her reactions always involved all her senses. Most of the time she even overreacted, but I always took that with a grain of salt. I figured, it's just how she is. But now, I'm not so sure. This might be too much, and I'm not sure if whether I should take this as a threat or just let it go, as something a bitter ex might say.

I check my watch again and I realize that I should hurry, unlesshurry unless I want to be late for my class. She kept me much longer than I thought. I try to push this incident out of my mind, and the moment I think of Ava, everything else seems to fade away. I don't know if this is what it feels like to be in love. Maybe it's just infatuation. Only, wouldn't that die out once you sleep with that someone? Sleeping with her only made my hunger for her greater and that's what's freaking me out.

I run to the main building, hoping to be able to see her soon.

Chapter Nine

Ava

"So, you really won't tell me what he's like in bed?"

I hear Sylvia's voice from the room, while I'm still in the bathroom, brushing my teeth. I pause to spit, thinking that if I chuckle with all that toothpaste foam in my mouth, I'll choke. I don't reply, proceeding to wash my face, gently patting it dry with a towel. When I open my eyes, she's standing in the doorway to the bathroom, staring at me.

"Come on," she urges again. "His skills are the stuff of legend."

"Then, what do you need me for when you and the whole university know everything about his lovemaking skills?" I chuckle, throwing the towel at her. She catches it right before it slams against her face.

"Listen to her, lovemaking," she rolls her eyes. "Guys like that don't make love, Ava. Don't forget that. It's all just sex to them."

I hate to admit it, but it's good advice. Sure, we had a good time, and he did say he'd call back to arrange a next date, but it's been two days and I haven't heard from him at all. I wanted to send him a casual message, but every time I start, I remind myself that I don't want to be that girl. If he wants me, then he'll have to be clear about it. If it was just about love making... sex, to be more precise, I guess, then that's fine, too. I did start liking him sort of, but it'll be alright even if I don't hear from him again.

That is at least what I'm trying to convince myself of. Sometimes it works, sometimes not. It depends on my mood, and whether Sylvia is there to actively remind me that he's an absolutely giver in bed and really does his best to make sure his partner is pleased. You can't fault him there.

"I know," I nod to Sylvia, as she moves to the side to let me out of the bathroom. "I haven't fallen in love with him or anything, if that's what you're afraid of."

"Haven't you?" She frowns, eyeing me like an old doctor who can pinpoint an ailment just by looking at the patient. "You seem pretty smitten by him."

"I do not," I shake my head. "I haven't been talking about him at all."

"My point exactly," she points her index finger at me.

"What are you talking about, you crazy woman?" I smile, as I sit on my bed. She walks over to hers, which rests against the opposite side of the wall.

"I'm saying that it's a big deal exactly because you don't want to talk about it. You're keeping it a secret, as if it's something important. Otherwise, you'd answer my question."

"You just wanna find out what exactly he does in the sack, admit it," I chuckle, grabbing a pillow from behind me and throwing it at her.

"Hey!" She catches it flying and throws it back at me. "Come on! Tell me!"

"No," I keep shaking my head at her, ready to fling to pillow at her again if she keeps insisting, but a loud knock on the door interrupts us.

"Come in!" Sylvia shouts, thinking it's probably Beth, who's attending the same class we're getting ready for, and is probably here to pick us up. Despite the invitation, the door stays closed, and no one enters. "Oh, come on," Sylvia grumbles as she gets up and walks to the door. "I hate it when people need a written permission to enter a room. Not like we have any privacy here anyway."

She opens the door, but from where I'm sitting, I can't see who it is.

"Hello?" Sylvia calls out, but I hear no reply. "Seriously? You're gonna do this elementary school bullshit of knocking on people's doors then just bale?"

I get up, curious as to what's happening, but when I join her in the doorway, I realize the hallway is empty. It's usually like this at this time of the morning, because most people are out in class. Our morning class was cancelled, which was why we're left among the last ones here.

"I don't see anyone," I say, more to myself than to her.

"No shit, Sherlock," she frowns, about to close the door, when I suddenly see a white envelope on the floor, right by the door.

"Wait, what's that?" I point at it, and she bends down to pick it up. When she turns it around, we both see it has my name on it. Just Ava. Nothing else.

"Are you expecting something?" Sylvia wonders, as we both enter, and she closes the door.

"No," I shake my head. "Nothing like this."

"Open it," she urges, yet my trembling fingers seem not to like that idea very much. Still, I do it. I extract a folded piece of paper. I started reading out loud.

Bluebells, cockle shells, Eevie, ivy over, I like coffee, I like tea. I like the boys and the boys like me. Tell your father to hold his tongue, he did something bad when he was young. Tell his father to do the same because they all forgot his name.

"What is this?" I wonder, realizing it's supposed to be a song of some sort, maybe a nursery rhyme.

"It's one of those old hopscotch songs," Sylvia recognizes it. "Give me the paper."

I do as she tells me, and she starts whispering something inaudible, nodding in rhythm as she does so.

"Yeah, it's a hopscotch song," she confirms. "Only, that's not the original version. I think it should be: tell your mother to hold her tongue, she had a fellow when she was young, tell your father to do the same, he had a girl, and he changed her name."

"Why would someone send me a rewritten old hopscotch song?" I frown, having absolutely no idea what this could possibly mean.

"There's no name?" She wonders, turning the paper over, inspecting it on all sides. "No. Nothing else. Just your name and this silly song. If we take it literally, someone thinks your father did something bad."

"My dad is the nicest guy ever," I jump to his defense. "He wouldn't hurt a fly. So, whoever thinks that is wrong."

"I believe you," Sylvia says defensively. "Just asking. There's another dad involved. Who's his dad?"

"No idea," I shrug.

"Could it be pretty boy's dad?" She asks.

"I doubt it," I shrug again. "I don't know his father."

"I think it's rubbish," she finally concludes, crumpling the paper in her hands. I want her to give it back to me, but I know there's no point. It doesn't matter what that is. Someone playing a stupid prank, I bet. Maybe some sorority or fraternity prank. "Don't pay attention to this, Ava. Focus on the pretty boy and getting at least one more night of sheer, unadulterated pleasure. Do it for the rest of us who can only dream of that..."

I chuckle at her presentation, when again, we are interrupted by my phone ringing. Sylvia pats her wrist with the tip of her index finger, indicating that we really need to get going, and I nod. I pick up the phone, because I see it's my dad.

"Hey, dad," I beam, welcoming his voice.

"Hey, sweetie," he replies, sounding cheerful, but a bit tired. "Did I catch you at a bad time?"

"Well, I'm about to head out to class with Sylvia, but I've got a few minutes, don't worry," I smile.

"I just wanted to hear our voice," he tells me. "Your mother and I miss you so much, sweetie."

"I miss you, too, dad," I reply. "I promise I'll come for a visit as soon as I can."

"I know you will. We know you have a life of your own, and sometimes, there are more pressing matters than visiting your parents, and we understand."

"No, dad," I assure him. "I appreciate the understanding, but I miss home too much to stay away from it for too long. Besides, you're not that far away. You could come for a visit any time you want."

"No, you know we don't want to impose, you've got your obligations there and we don't want to distract you from your studies."

Sylvia taps her wrist again, and I nod. "I promise we'll see each other soon. Whether it's me going or you coming over here, we'll make it happen. Say hi to mom. I'm sorry, but I really need to get going."

"Of course, sweetie," he says apologetically. "Call us when you can."

"I'll call tonight before bedtime."

"Deal," he says. "Have a nice day, sweetheart. We love you."

"Love you, too, guys. Bye."

I hang up the phone, and quickly put on a pullover, jumping into a pair of jeans, and I'm done.

"What if you run into Mr. Hot Pants?" She asks, and I chuckle at the name we used to refer to him by before. It suits him perfectly, even now. Maybe especially now.

"It's me who's the hot pants now," I joke, turning around and working my butt, which makes me burst out laughing.

"Just... do anything but that, and you'll be fine," she winks at me, as we both grab our backpacks and head out, picking up Beth on the way.

We all chat as we head to class, and I appreciate that Sylvia doesn't mention Gabriel even once. It's not that I'm adamant on keeping him a secret. I just like to keep my private business... well, private. Especially with him. Everyone knows him. I don't want to be just another tick in his little black book. But, according to Sylvia, that is exactly what I am.

My mind accepts that with strange serenity, and I realize it's only because it's focused on something else. That note. It's still making me anxious, for more reasons than one. Who sent it? More importantly, why? And who are the fathers in the stupid song? Does my dad really have something to do with this? I can't believe that. I know my dad.

I try to convince myself that it's just a stupid prank, and nothing more. I'm ridiculous dwelling on it for so long. Sylvia probably forgot all about it already.

That's because it wasn't her name on the envelope...

I try my best to focus on class, but it's impossible. Someone wanted me to get that letter and read that song. Someone wants me to know something, to find out something. But what?

Chapter Ten

Gabriel

Pick you up tonight at 9 then.

I consider adding a kiss emoji to this, but quickly change my mind. I don't want to be cheesy or anything even remotely like that. I was hoping I could take her out to the movies, but she told me that she needed to do some research for her project, and she always does it in the library. I told her that she's the only person I know who still finds use for that old, dilapidated building. I imagine her smiling at the message. She replied with a wink. So, nine it is.

I put away my phone and check the time. It's fifteen minutes past two. My dad is fifteen minutes late, which according to his time measurement, is hours and hours late. I consider calling him but decide against it. Instead, I call for the waiter, who brings me the menu and I order what my dad usually has for lunch. It's fish on Mondays, veal on Tuesdays, sushi on Wednesdays, lamb on Thursday, no meat Friday, and weekends are up to his whim. Most of the time, he doesn't even have lunch on the weekends, because he locks himself up in his study at home, and spends hours there, without lifting his head from the computer screen.

During work hours, his lunches are usually work lunches. They are ingrained into his daily work schedule, so he can't skip them, unless he wants his business to suffer. After all, the Emerald Price Industries owe all their success to one man and one man alone: my father. Still, such grand success doesn't come without certain sacrifices. I knew that my father has subjected everything to his company, even his personal and family life. Now that his wife was gone and his son is a grown up, there is nothing else left to focus on but the company, which my father assured him me would eventually be mine.

Honestly, I've had conflicting feelings about that. I've seen what that company has done to my father. I've seen how it has demanded everything from him, and I'm not sure that's what I want for myself. Sure, the money came in handy, but is money really all that is to it?

At that moment, I lift my gaze and see my father approaching the table. As always, he is immaculately dressed, his cufflinks shining around his wrist. He sits down, and the waiter flies over, to pour him a glass of wine. My father covers the top of his glass with his hand.

"None for me, thank you," he shakes his head. I look at him curiously. "I had a meeting until three am last night."

"Why so late?" I wonder.

"Different time zones," he explains. "If I take even a single sip of wine, I'm afraid I'll fall asleep during my next meeting, which is in exactly…" He lifts his wrist to check his golden Rolex. "Fifty-five minutes."

I've stopped being upset over these times lunches a long time ago. I figured, if that is the only way to see him and have some quality time with him, so be it.

"Sorry, I'm late," he adds, then turns to the waiter. "I'll have– "

"I already ordered for you," I tell him.

"Yes, your dishes are coming right up," the waiter confirms.

"In that case, I'll just take an Evian."

"Yes, sir," the waiter nods, then leaves.

"Big day today?" I ask, although that question could be asked of my father on any given day.

"Too many meetings this week," he admits to something I've never heard him say. "But I don't want to talk about work. I want to talk about you. Tell me what's new with you."

"Nothing much," I shrug, as always.

He lifts his eyebrow inquisitively at me. "And that girl?"

"I saw her again," I admit, with a revealing smile.

"Getting serious then, is it?" He ends the question with a high note, sounding as if he's extremely amused by all this. I'm also glad, because he's usually never taken much interest in my love life. Maybe because

I'm older now, and he still thinks I should settle down soon. Maybe he's right.

"She's difficult to decipher," I confess. "Sometimes, I don't know where I stand with her."

"But that makes her different, doesn't it?" He hits the bull's eye with that one.

"She's unlike any other girl I've ever met," I say, like a broken record.

"You know what Coco Chanel said?" He asks me, and I remember then it was mom who loved her. "In order to be irreplaceable, one must always be different. It would seem that this mystery girl of yours has made herself quite irreplaceable."

I chuckle at his analogy, and I must admit, it is totally true. I can't imagine myself seeing any other girl right now. The more time passes by, the more convinced I am that I might never need any other at all. The thought is both thrilling and frightening at the same time.

"What does she look like, this mysterious girl of yours?"

"Wait, I can show you," I gabgrab my phone again, and skim through the photos in my phone.

Ava has no social media. I learned that the hard way. But she did allow me to take a photo of the two of us, only after I insisted several times, and she realized she wouldn't be able to say no.

I find it among a sea of other photos I have absolutely no need or use from, and I turn the phone to my father. I expect him to have something clever to say again, but the moment he sees her, the smile disappears from his face. He grabs the phone from my hand, and brings it closer to his eyes, as if to inspect it better.

"Is everything alright?" I ask, wondering what's the going on and why this strange reaction. He doesn't say anything. His eyes widen, then squint, then widen again. I notice his Adam's apple bob up then down, as if he swallowed very heavily.

The waiter comes and leaves two plates of food on our table, but neither of us even thinks about eating right now. He's watching her photo, and I'm watching him, waiting for any explanation that might shed some light on this. Finally, he looks up at me.

"You need to break it off, immediately."

His voice is harsh. It's a complete contrast to the tone which he had mere moments ago, not to mention what he's been telling me, how he was all happy about me finding someone special. Was that all a lie? It sure seems so.

"What?" I frown, not finding the right words to even start questioning this comment he just made. "Why?"

"I can't explain it right now," he says, giving me the phone back, as if he just got severely burned by it and doesn't want to be anywhere near it. "You have to trust me."

"I do trust you, dad, but... what's going on? Seriously?"

He sighs, squinting once, very hard, as he presses the bridge of his nose. Then, he blinks heavily several times, finally focusing his gaze once more on me.

"I can't tell you," he repeats, as if I haven't heard it the first time.

"So, you're just going to leave me with that?" I ask, dumbfounded. "You don't even know her."

"I know her..." He starts but stops himself. I feel like there would have been something else to end that statement. Her what? Her family? Her reputation? All sorts of crazy ideas pop to mind, one more unbelievable than the other.

"You're probably mistaking her for someone," I try the least crazy explanation I can think of. But the look on his face doesn't change. I see those deep lines becoming deeper with each passing second. It is as if in mere moments, he has grown older. Like ten years older. "Maybe someone you used to know?"

He falls silent for a while, then nods. "You're probably right." He tries to smile, but it's a weak effort, barely successful. I'm not buying it.

"Probably?" I wonder.

"I'm an old man, Gabriel," he tells me with a sigh. "Every old man, especially a man as successful as I am, has made a few enemies here and there. I guess she just reminded me of someone I haven't thought about in a long while."

"A woman?" I ask, and immediately, an affair pops to mind. "Don't tell me you cheated on mom."

"What?" He is genuinely shocked at the insinuation, and for that, I am relieved. "Don't be absurd. I haven't looked at any other woman while your mother was alive, not even after she left us."

I lower my gaze, feeling bad for even having insinuated it. "I'm sorry."

"It's alright," he assures me. "My reaction was inappropriate. It's merely that her face triggered an unpleasant memory, which of course has nothing to do with her. She just reminds me of someone, that's all. Can we just forget all about this and enjoy our meal?" He smiles, successfully this time.

"Sure thing, dad," I nod, watching him take the fork and knife and dig into his veal. I do the same.

We exchange a few more pleasantries, both of us consciously focusing on the current conversation, not wanting to step back into the conversation that almost ruined our lunch.

Yet, that is all I can think about. His reaction was completely atypical. I don't remember if he's ever reacted to someone or something so rashly, so strangely, and that has made me all the more curious to find out more about this memory. Only, I doubt he'd want to share anything about it. Maybe the key lies in his past. But where to start?

"Well, I should get going now," he tells me after a quick glance at his watch. He raises his hand to call the waiter, but I stop him.

"I'll take care of the bill," I explain. "I want to have a quick coffee before I head back, and they made the best espresso in town here."

"I'd love to join you, Gabriel," he smiles, "but, if I stay a minute longer, I fear I might be late to my next meeting."

"Sure thing," I smile back. "I understand."

Of course, I do. What I don't understand is his reaction.

"Are you sure you're OK?" I ask, realizing that I should probably just leave it be and forget all about it. But I want to know about that mysterious memory and why is it haunting him like this.

He immediately turns grave, then nods. "I'm fine. That is not something I wish to discuss, Gabriel, and I hope you can respect my privacy."

"Yes, of course," I promise him.

But it's not a promise I intend to keep. I watch him as he leaves the restaurant, then I grab my phone again. I gaze at Ava's smiling face, her slightly blushing cheeks, her bouncy curls framing that sweet, heart-shaped face. How could anyone react like that to her?

Just let it go.

The voice is right. It's probably none of my business. Whatever it is, it belongs in my father's past, and that is probably where it should stay. I should leave well enough alone.

I order a coffee for myself, and at that moment, she messages back. Looking forward to it. Plus, the winking face.

I grin at the phone. She can make me forget about anything.

Chapter Eleven

Ava

Finally, the last lecture for the day is over, and I head back to my dorm. It's still early in the evening, so despite the night lights already being turned on, there are a lot of people still hanging out on the benches and the grass. A part of me remembers what happened a few nights ago, but I try not to let it dictate the way I feel about this place. This is where I should feel safe, and no one will take that feeling away from me.

I enter my dorm and see a familiar face. "Hey!" I smile. "Clayton, right?"

"Yes," he smiles back. "Eva?"

"Ava," I correct him. "But that's close enough."

He chuckles. "Everything good?"

"Yes," I nod, deciding not even to ask about that strange letter I received. Even I did ask him, what could he possibly know about it? The doors here are open for anyone with a coded key card. I've even seen the door left jammed open, so anyone could come in, even without the card. I personally don't mind. But that only means that Clayton or any other guard couldn't possibly even begin to tell who might be leaving weird letters to people in the dorm. Namely, me.

"Any special plans for the evening?" He wonders.

"No," I shake my head. "My roommate is off at her boyfriend's place, so I get the whole place to myself. That doesn't happen very often, so I plan on taking advantage of the chance."

"Carpe diem, huh?" He winks at me.

"You know it," I nod, thinking he is pretty clever for a night guard.

Realizing that I'm starting to overthink things again, as I often have a tendency to do, I wave at him and head for the stairs. "Good night, Clayton."

"Good night, Miss. Ava."

"Ava will do," I turn around, to point at him with my index finger, then head back to my room. I pass by a few familiar faces on the way there, then finally reach my door. I expect it to be locked, as we always lock it when no one's in, and I'm surprised to see it push open on its own the moment I try to put the key in the lock.

What I see before me makes me expel a silent gasp. I press my hand to my lips as my gaze falls across all the stuff that's been thrown across the room. I see all my clothes, socks, underwear, all my papers, books, pillows, the bed linens. Everything is out. In this mess, I can't even tell if something is missing or not, but then again, I didn't have anything of value in here. I always take my laptop with me, as I do my wallet with my cards. So, whatever this person was looking for, I bet he or she didn't find it.

At this point, I'm wondering if all three things are connected somehow: me being followed, the strange letter and now this. But how are they all connected? What's going on here? The fact I don't have any answers is only making me more exhausted and more anxious. At least it's a good thing Sylvia wasn't here. Who knows what could have happened if she was in the room when this person came looking for God knows what.

I walk down the stairs and back to Clayton, who is reading a book. He lifts his gaze immediately upon hearing the sound of oncoming footsteps.

"Miss... "" he starts, then stops. "Ava," he corrects himself. "Changed your mind about a peaceful night alone?"

"Someone changed my mind for me," I frown.

I feel the cold talon of fear tapping my shoulder, but I pay no attention to it. I refuse to. No one can harm me here. I am safe, although someone has made it his or her mission to prove otherwise.

"What do you mean?"

"I think someone broke into my room," I start a conversation I never thought I'd be having. "I mean, I know someone broke into my room."

"Did they steal anything?" He immediately jumps from his post and heads over closer to me.

"I don't think so," I shrug. "But honestly, it's such a mess, I can't tell if anything is missing. Sylvia should take a look, too, but I don't want to worry her about this now."

"Well, if something like that happened, I'm afraid we need to contact the police," he tells me. "Just in case."

"Sure," I nod. I don't like the idea of having to talk to them, but maybe whoever did this sees the policemen, and freaks out a little. Maybe he or she will then stop. At least, I'm hoping that's what's going to happen.

He walks over to his desk and calls 911. I listen to him explain what happened, then he nods a few times and finally says OK, thank you. He lifts his gaze to mine again. "They should be here in half an hour."

"OK," I nod again, with a heavy sigh.

"They said not to go inside until they come."

"I immediately noticed what happened when I got in, and I immediately went back out, without touching anything."

"That's good," he confirms. "While we're waiting, maybe you'd like a coffee or something?" He asks a little nervously.

"No, thank you," I shake my head. "I just want to get this over with. This isn't how I imagined my night at all."

His lips part for him to say something, but he's interrupted by the sound of my cell ringing. I reply immediately seeing who it is.

"Hey," I greet him, mustering the last morsels of joy I have left. But he sees right through it.

"Hey," he repeats. "How was your day?" That's a question I didn't expect.

"I was nice, it just didn't end very nicely," I give him an honest reply.

"What happened?"

"Someone broke into my room."

"Are you OK?" He asks immediately. "I'll come right over."

"No, you don't have to," I say, but I'm touched by the sheer knowledge that he'd drop whatever it is he's doing to come over. "I'm here with Clayton and– "

"Who's Clayton?" He asks, sounding just a tad bit jealous, and I know it's wrong, but I like it.

"The night guard here at the dorm," I explain. "He called the police and now we're waiting for them."

"I'm coming over, Ava."

"Gabriel, you don't have to," I urge him. "It'll probably be a pain in the ass."

"No, seriously, Ava," I listen to him say. "I'm coming to help you with whatever it is you need, and then I'm bringing you back to my place. You're not spending the night there."

"No, I– "

"Ava, when are you going to stop pushing me away?" He asks, and that is yet another question I don't understand.

I look up at Clayton. He immediately turns away, embarrassed that I caught his eye looking in my direction, as if he's been listening in on my conversation. So, I turn around and take a few steps away from him.

"I'm not pushing you away," I say more to say something than to make a point. In fact, he's right. I have been pushing him away, but that is just because I'm afraid of admitting what I'm feeling for him. What if he ends up hurting me? I don't want to get hurt. It's easier just to remove oneself from such a situation slowly and painlessly.

"You are," he convinces me. "Don't lie. Ava, I won't hurt you."

Damn his ability to read my mind.

"You can't make such promises," I whisper into the receiving end of my cell.

"I can, and I will. Just let me be there for you."

I sigh. It's probably not a good idea to stay in my room tonight anyway. I doubt whoever's been there would be returning, knowing that Clayton will be keeping an eye out on any suspicious activities, but still. Maybe I should let Gabriel be what he wants to be for me, and just see where it leads.

"OK," I finally say."

"OK?" He repeats.

"Yes, you parrot," I chuckle. "Come here then, and when I'm done with the police, you can take me back to your place. I feel like having a pizza."

"Pizza it is," he agrees. "I'm coming right over, won't take me longer than fifteen minutes."

"You know where to find me," I smile. "Bye."

I hang up the phone, and when I turn around, I see Clayton is busy with something on his desk.

"Boyfriend?" He suddenly asks, noticing I'm done with my conversation.

"Sort of," I shrug. "It's complicated."

Then, he tells me something I didn't even know was true. "It shouldn't be."

I think about it for a few moments, then I nod. "You're right. And, you know what else? I think I'll have a hot chocolate or something. Coffee will just make me jittery. I'll go get it from the machine. You want something?"

"A coffee," he smiles. "Thanks."

"Sure thing."

I walk over for our drinks, with his words echoing in my mind. It shouldn't be. He's right. He's absolutely right. Why do we always make simple situations so difficult?

Chapter Twelve

Gabriel

It's close to two am when we finally get back to my apartment. The drive back was silent. Ava fell asleep in the car, but the moment I tried to pick her up in my arms and get her upstairs, her eyes pop open. For a moment, it seems she's forgotten where she is and why she isn't sleeping in her own bed.

"Sorry," I smile awkwardly. "You fell asleep, so I figured, I'd just take you upstairs and put you to bed."

She is listening to me, but there is such an incredulous look on her face and it's making me doubt my own sincerity, as if she's doubting it, too. It saddens me to see that she is consciously building up a wall between us. I know I don't seem like the most trustworthy guy, but if only she'd let me show her my true self, she would see so much more to me than what everyone else keeps assuming.

I know my track record. I never thought it would work against me, but the day did come. No matter what I tell her, she has a mind of her own, and she will only believe what she herself thinks. That's what you get for choosing a girl who's got a good head on her shoulders. I've been fine with the others before, but only when I met her, did I realize that I've been in need of something more meaningful, something I can hold on to.

"I'll walk, thanks," she says, accepting my hand to get out of the car. At least that.

We go up in silence, and she enters my apartment after I open the door, finding a cozy spot on my sofa, right where she was last time she was here. My cock springs to action, at the mere thought of what happened between us. She tasted so sweet. My tongue is aching to taste her again, but I don't want to take advantage of this. I didn't bring her back here to fuck her. I brought her here because I have no idea what's going on, and before we do find out, I don't want to let her out of my sight.

"Are you OK?" I ask, seeing her lost in thought.

She doesn't reply for a few moments, and I allow her to settle back into reality and the present moment. "I'm fine, just…" She looks up, not staring at me, but through me, somewhere into the distance behind me, through the wall, through the darkness outside. "Weird things have been happening."

"Weird?" I repeat, remembering my dad's reaction to her photo. "What do you mean weird?"

"Well, a few weeks back, I thought someone was following me when I was returning from the library one evening," she admits. "I didn't really see anyone, you know. I just had a feeling, and I thought I heard someone whisper my name, but you know what darkness and a tired mind can do to your psyche. They create things that aren't there. Clayton checked that evening and the following days, but he says no one complained of the same and he didn't see any suspicious people around. So, I brushed it off."

"But?" I sense there's more coming, and sure enough, she continues.

"Then, I received a weird letter with a hopscotch song written on it."

"A hopscotch song?" I repeat, wondering if I've heard it well. "Like the game?"

"Yes, like the game. Only, it's changed a bit, and mentions my father and his father."

"Whose father?"

"His," she shrugs. "Only I have no idea who he is."

I swallow heavily. She mentioned his father. Could that someone be referring to my father? But what do my father and her father have in common? I doubt they even know each other. How could they?

"So, those were the two things which I just let go, because I figured someone must be pulling my leg, or I don't know... doing this for initiation into a fraternity or a sorority? I mean, I've heard of them being forced to do weird stuff like this, I wouldn't be surprised by it."

"I know what you mean," I nod. "I've also heard very strange initiation stories."

"Right?" She looks up at me, hopeful.

I've never seen her like this. She wants the world to see her as a tough nut no one can crack, but in fact, she is the exact opposite. She is a kind, gentle soul who needs someone to understand her.

I lean over to her, and the desire to kiss her is overwhelming. Still, I resist it. I need to tell her what happened with my father. Maybe together we can shed some light on this, although I can't possibly begin to comprehend what we could ever have in common, or our fathers for that matter.

"I uhm... I showed my dad your photo," I start, not sure how she would take this. The last thing I want to do is scare her off, but at the same time, I want her to be completely sure that this isn't just a fling for me. It's so much more, more than even I myself am willing to admit. "You know, the one we took together?" I add casually. She just looks at me, waiting for me to continue. "And, he had a very strange reaction to your photo."

She knits her eyebrow in surprise. "What do you mean strange? He doesn't even know me."

"Right?" I point at her with my index finger, in need of doing something physical with my body while I shared this odd story. "My thoughts exactly. He turned pale, telling me we shouldn't see each other, but then, as if he himself realized how strange all that sounded, he came up with this excuse that you just reminded him of someone very much, and it was an unpleasant memory, so that was why he reacted like that."

"Well... I guess that makes sense," she tells me. "Doesn't it?"

"It did, but in light of these new developments, I can't help but wonder if all these things are connected somehow."

"Our two families?" Her nose turns upward at the idea.

"I don't mean like the two of us being relatives or anything like that, God no!" The thought makes me gag. It can't be that. "No, I think it's something else."

"I can't imagine my father hiding anything from me," she tells me, completely sure of herself. As for me, I wish I had such reassurance. My father has had his fair secrets in his life, but none of them affected me. Until now.

"Not to burst your bubble, but parents are human, just like the rest of us, and as such, they have flaws and sometimes, even secrets. I learned that the hard way around the time my mom passed."

"Your mom passed?" She repeats, turning to me, her voice tender and caring. "I'm so sorry, I didn't know."

"It happened a while back," I shrug. "I've dealt with it when I needed to. Now, she is just a warm presence in the back of my mind, like a soft glow to every childhood memory I have."

"That was so nicely put, poetic almost."

"I'm not just a stupid jock, you know," I grin. "Although you did peg me for one."

"OK, I admit," she giggles. Then suddenly, she turns serious again. "But, as for our previous conversation, I don't know what your dad is hiding, but mine is an open book."

"If that's the case, I'm glad," I say with every bit of sincerity I have left. "I just feel like every man who attended this university and who became a big shot of some sort, has some secrets to hide."

Then, she says it. "My dad attended this university as well. He's not a big shot, especially not compared to your father, but we're doing alright, and like I said, he's got not secrets to hide."

"Wait... go back," I quickly say. "Your father went to this university, too?"

"Yes," she nods. "Why?"

"When was that?"

"Wait..." she thinks about it for a few moments. "I think from 1975 to 1980, or something like that."

I feel like someone has finally pulled the curtain from off my eyes, and things are slowly falling into place.

"Then, odds are he knows my dad, because my dad attended in that exact same period."

We fall silent immediately, hesitating to say anything. We found the connection that we've been looking for. But even if they did know each other, what does that prove? There must be more to this, something we still don't see.

"What do you think all this means?" She asks.

I want to give her a straight answer, but all I can do is sigh. I don't know what to tell her. I'm as lost and confused as she is.

"It could mean nothing, just a coincidence," I tell her, although it's obvious neither of us is buying this.

"No, there has to be more to this," she echoes my own thoughts from a moment ago.

"Well, there's no point wracking our brains over this at 2 am," I tell her. "Especially after you found out someone broke into your room."

"We're just lucky neither me nor Sylvia were there."

"Do you think something could have happened if you were there?" The thought makes my blood boil, someone hurting her in any way.

"I don't know," she admits. "But we can't rule it out."

I don't want to say it out loud, but she's right. We can't rule anything out at this point.

"It's been a long day," I get up from the sofa reluctant to give up my place next to her, but she needs to sleep. She's had quite a day and the last thing she needs is me breathing down her neck. "You should go to bed. I just want you to know that I'm trying to give you all the space you need to sort out whatever you need to sort out, but also know that I'm here for anything you need, Ava. Anything."

She stands up and approaches me, the tips of her fingers finding my lips and opening them gently.

"I want you..." She whispers.

All the blood in my body rushes to one place. Hearing her say this makes me unable to think straight, and I can't even ask her if she's really sure. I lift her up into my arms and take her to bed. She kisses me immediately, hungrily, and I know that I'm way over my head with this girl, but all I can do is just keep kissing her.

Chapter Thirteen

Ava

Our kisses are even hungrier this time than before, as if the first time we slept together merely opened up a huge, insatiable well of need and desire, and no matter how much we fed it, it kept being hungrier and hungrier. He doesn't taste like wine. This time, it is only him. It is only he who has the ability to steal my breath like this, to make my heart pound a million times in a minute.

I chase away the heaviness still lingering in my mind, by pulling his face closer to my own. He wastes no time in responding to my kisses, as he drops me playfully on the bed, hovering over me on all fours, like a beast of the jungle, ready to pounce on its prey.

His kisses are magical. They manage to make me forget all about my worries and concerns. The whole world fell apart around us, with the only thing standing strong being the two of us, lost in our own little world. There is nothing for me to do but feel the ecstasy he's throwing me into.

I don't know if this moment is all we have, but I know that I'm greedy for him. I want to please him, to make him feel everything that's he's never felt with anyone else, because that is exactly what he has been doing for me. My hand slides down his pants. His bulge is undeniable. The knowledge that he wants me as much as I want him only strengthens my desire for him. My fingers curl around his bulge, feeling it. He groans into my ear.

I find his lips again, nipping at them. His breathing is shallow, ragged. He pulls away to look at me, with only a little bit of light shining upon us from the small lamp in the corner. His eyes are fathomless, wanting to tear down all the walls I've built around me, and that's dangerous.

"Take me," I whisper.

"You're mine," he says in a guttural tone, and all I can do is agree.

He kisses me more soundly this time, our clothes fly around the room, in the pauses of us kissing. I giggle when he fumbles with my bra, unable to unhook it immediately.

"You are so fucking gorgeous," his gaze burning into mine.

His face falls over mine, stealing my laughter and leaving a throbbing need in its place. I've never felt this desirable, this cherished, not until this very moment with him. I feel like he managed to light up a forgotten candle inside of me, and now, not only is it burning, but it is threatening to set everything ablaze.

"I've been waiting for days to touch you," he murmurs, and heat pools between my thighs, as his hand finds my breast, fondling it. "To kiss you. I... I can't get enough of you..."

I want to tell him that I know the feeling, but he's stolen my breath. He's stolen everything I hold dearest to me, and all I can do is keep offering more. I inhale deeply, his scent musky and delicious. His hand trails down my body, finding my wetness. My fingers are pressed against his tight, warm flesh. It feels like he's made of solid rock underneath. The ache between my thighs is undeniable, and I know I can't take much more of this.

My hand ravels down his rock hardrock-hard abs, all the way to his throbbing cock, pulsing with desire. I wrap my fingers around it. Tonight, it belongs to me. I didn't even know how much I wanted him, until I felt him in my hand, on my skin, inside of me. Yes, I want him inside of me again and again.

"I need you," I whisper to him, without the slightest trace of embarrassment or shame. One should never be ashamed of one's feelings, and I've only been sharing mine with him.

"Yes, darling..." He whispers back in a tone I don't expect, but I welcome, nonetheless. He sounds more loving than I ever thought he could be.

I become frenzied, my desire completely taking over. He pulls down my panties. Now, we're both naked. I am showered with more kisses, soft nibbles, tugging at my lower lip, and all I can do is moan loudly, waiting for that moment when I shall become undone. But once again, like the previous time, he is torturing me by taking his time. I can't have my fill of him, and neither can he.

I reach again for his cock, squeezing it, stroking it from the root, enjoying his size and the thumping sensation. My finger trails an invisible line over the velvety softness of his skin, finding the tip which is already beading with desire.

"I don't know how long I'll be able to last if you keep doing that to me, you tease," he murmurs right into my ear, his hot breath spilling all over my neck, sending goosebumps up and down my body.

He pulls away, his cock disappearing from my hand, leaving an emptiness that was insatiable. I'm becoming greedy now. Gentle caresses won't do any longer. My body is desperately impatient. I need him. My thighs quiver, as he lowers his head right between them. All I can do is obey his silent guidance, releasing a gut-wrenching moan as soon as his tongue touched my pulsing flesh. My whole body is trembling in anticipation, as he keeps sucking on my clit, his fingers sliding into me, curling at just the right angle. I thrust my hips closer to him, as his other hand slides up to my breast, cupping it, his thumb working my nipple.

I close my eyes, allowing the sensation to wash over me. The trembling, all-encompassing explosion lifts me off the bed and I feel like I'm about to come undone. Still quivering with the remnants of my orgasm, he turns me around, propping me up on my knees. I hear the familiar sound of the wrapper opening, and within seconds, he plunges deep inside of me, stretching me, filling me. It's the most divine sensation I've ever felt. He grabs my hair, pulling be me backward, arching my back, his hand slapping my butt, which evokes a stinging sensation which perfectly pairs up with the pleasure that only seems to heighten.

He is pumping faster and faster, our movements becoming furious, unstoppable. His fingers find my clit once again, and all it takes is one gentle press in the right place, and I swallow the scream of my second orgasm. He cums immediately afterwards, slumping down onto me, breathing heavily.

A moment later, we both roll to the side, his arms wrapped around me, our hearts pounding in perfect unison. None of us says anything for a while, and I think he's fallen asleep. I try to get up to grab a blanket.

"You're not thinking of going again, are you?" I hear him ask.

I've considered it. A war has been waging between my mind and my heart, and finally, my heart has won. Maybe it's OK to give him a chance, even at the risk of hurting me somewhere along the line. Hiding away one's heart is never the answer. How does that awful, cheesy saying go? Better to have loved and lost, than never to have loved at all? I chuckle at my own silly thoughts.

"Did I say anything funny?" He wonders.

"No, no," I shake my head, turning to him only to kiss him softly on the forehead. "I'm just... lost in thought."

"You're not regretting what happened?" He asks, propping himself up on his elbows. I can hear the concern in his voice. I feel overwhelmed by tenderness, because I see a boy before me who wants to be loved, not a jock who wants to be the center of attention. I wonder which of the two is the real Gabriel Price. Maybe it's worth sticking around to find out.

"Definitely not," I assure him. "In fact, I'm not regretting it so much that I'll actually spend the night here."

"You will?" He wonders, as if he hasn't expected me to say that.

"Yes... I mean, if that's OK..." I add quickly, not wanting to impose, unless he wants me to stay. Then, that's different.

"Stay," he tells me loud and clear. That's all I need.

"OK then," I smile, pulling the cover up to us and covering our naked bodies with it. I move closer to him, skin to skin, scorching hot. My knee falls over his thigh, and his hand cups my butt cheek. I expect him to make a move again, seeing he's touching me like that, but he doesn't. Instead, he just pecks me gently on the cheek, pulls me closer, and closes his eyes.

"I can take you to this awesome little French bakery just around the corner," he tells me, his voice sleepy and his eyes closed, but he's still there, still awake. "We can have breakfast there."

I remember then that I sent a message to Sylvia telling her to meet me at the café for a morning coffee before she heads back to our dorm room. I wanted to tell her in person what happened, but I also didn't want to ruin her night. It was bad enough that one of us had her night ruined.

I glance over at him. His breathing has become steady, his hand loosened its grip around me. Maybe my night wasn't really ruined. In fact, I wouldn't call it ruined at all. If that someone didn't break into my dorm room, I wouldn't have ended up here.

I smile in the darkness. Fate works in mysterious ways, bringing people together who didn't even think they would ever be this close. I couldn't shake the feeling that boundaries were crossed this evening. And these boundaries were the ones I myself have set up. Now that they were crossed, I fear that things will never again be the same.

The strangest thing about it all? I welcome the thought of the future, as it is, with him.

Chapter Fourteen

Gabriel

I don't know what time it is when the sound of the doorbell wakes me up. I pretend that I don't hear it, and turn to the side, only to find out that I'm the only person in the bed. Last night, there were two of us. I lift my head up immediately, her absence completely waking me up. I see no sign of her anywhere. Her clothes aren't on the floor anymore. It's as if last night was only a dream.

Someone presses on the doorbell again, and it rings for an eternity.

"I'm coming!" I shout as loud as I can.

I put on a pair of sweatpants on the way to the door, not caring one bit that I'm not wearing a t-shirt. Whoever it is must know that it's early and that it's Saturday morning. People like to sleep in. Especially people who stayed up late last night.

A part of me is still searching for Ava's presence in the apartment as I walk to the front door, but the whole place is more silent than a graveyard. Maybe it's her behind the door? She went somewhere, and is now back? My heart and my cock share the enthusiasm for this wish, as I unlock the door. My smile immediately disappears upon seeing who it was.

"Did I catch you at a bad time?" Ashley speaks seductively, and I notice her gazing somewhere behind me, in an effort to see whether there's someone else in the apartment, too.

"Yeah, I was sleeping," I inform her officially, without the slightest intention of inviting her in, although I'm guessing that's why she's standing here right now.

"Did I wake you up?" She asks innocently. "I didn't mean to."

"Never mind," I shrug. "Why are you here?"

"I'm here…" She takes a strand of her hair and starts swirling it around her index finger. "Because I don't like the way we parted last time."

The promises she made me about not leaving me alone? Hell yeah, I remember those. But so many things have taken precedence over it that I've barely thought about her or that.

"I understand," I sigh. "You were upset."

"I was," she agrees.

"That's fine."

"No, it's not fine," she corrects me. "I need to apologize."

"OK."

I'm still half-asleep, wondering where Ava has gone off to, and I'm really not interested in any apologies Ashley has to offer. But at the same time, I don't want to be an asshole. If she wants to apologize, sure, I'll hear her out. Anything just so that she leaves me alone.

"I shouldn't have spoken to you like that," she continues. "I was upset, but that doesn't give me the right."

"That's OK, Ash," I even manage a smile this time. "I'm just happy that things won't be awkward between us." I realize that it's not very nice making her stand in the doorway, when she's trying to apologize and make things right. "Why don't you come in, and I can make us both a coffee?" I step aside, and she immediately walks in.

"Make yourself comfortable," I urge. "I'll just go throw something on."

"You don't have to on my account," she shouts from the living room.

I pretend not to have heard that, walking into my bedroom and opening my wardrobe. At that very moment, I feel her hands slide around my waist, and try to grab my dick, but I manage to grab her by the wrist before she does it.

"What are you doing?" I turn around to face her, and she's got that same seductive smile she's always had, which she's obviously been hiding for the last five minutes.

"Isn't it obvious?" She purrs, only I want nothing to do with her. Inviting her in was a mistake. I see that now. But how the hell am I going to get her out now without a scene?

"I already told you, Ash," I remind her. "We won't be doing this anymore."

"Why? We were so good," she murmurs, getting closer to me, but I just step back, keeping a safe distance between us, now that I've let go of her wrist.

"We were, but you knew what to expect from me and what not to expect," I remind her.

"Is it because of her?" She suddenly asks.

"Who?" I squint at her. Did she find out about Ava?

"The girl who sneaked out this morning."

"When... how do you know about that?" I'm incredulous. That means she's been in front of my apartment building for at least an hour before she finally decided to wake me up.

"That doesn't matter," she leans over closer to me, her hand scorching my cheek. "None of that matters. I understand you needed to be with someone else, just to get that out of your system. But I also know that you will eventually grow bored of her, like you grow bored of every other girl you slept with, but me."

I want to correct her assumption, but I bet that will only make things worse, so I bite my tongue. I'm already in enough trouble as it is. I'm just waiting for her to continue, because she seems ready for a monologue.

"Can't you see, Gabriel?" She keeps talking, but at least she removes her hand from my face. She is staring into my eyes, and I can't help but think she's gone batshit crazy. "I'm the one for you. I've always been the one, only you can't see it. So, I have to show you. I am the one who understand your needs, your wants, no one else knows you like I do."

"Listen, Ashley..." I start, only I have no idea what to say. I've never dealt with an obsessed chick like this one. Whatever I do, I know I should tread carefully. "You are a lovely girl, and you are going to make a guy very happy, but unfortunately, that won't be me."

"It has to be you," she shakes her head, like a child that has been denied her favorite plaything. "No one else will ever do."

"I know that's what it seems like now, but trust me, this is just obsession, nothing else..."

"Obsession?" Her eyes flare up at me, her cheeks reddening. "This isn't obsession, it's love! I love you, Gabriel! Isn't that obvious to you? Who else would take you after you brought this girl home and fucked her all night long? Who else? Me! Just me!"

Fucking hell. Inviting her in was a cardinal mistake. If only I ended the conversation right there in the doorway, which would have allowed me to send her off without any drama. Now, between the safety of my apartment walls, she can shout and scream all she wants, and I doubt getting rid of her would be a piece of cake.

"You... "" Her voice quivers as she approaches me with her arms outstretched, and she cups my face with her palms. "You have to know how much I love you... you have to..."

"I know, Ashley, I know," I assure her.

"Tell me you love me, too," she insists. "You do love me, don't you?"

I wrap my fingers around her wrists, just in case. You never know how women like this might react, and it's not wise to have their nails anywhere near your face.

"I do love you, I really do," I nod softly, "only not in the way you want me to. You are a very good, dear friend, and that's what you'll always be." I'm lying, but none of that matters now. I just want her out of my house. "If you need help, just tell me what to do and I'll do it." This one isn't a lie. I feel sorry for her, but I still want her out.

"But... you are the love of my life," her voice is still trembling.

I can see a few tears rolling down her face, and I feel like a bastard.

"Can I have a hug?" She asks.

"Sure," I nod, wrapping my arms around her. She rests her head on my chest, and inhales deeply.

We stay like that for a while, and I don't want to be the first one to break it, although I feel all sorts of awkward and uncomfortable about this. Still, I don't want to throw her out as if she was nobody to me. She is still a friend, and I see now that mixing the boundaries between a friend and a friend with benefits can sometimes backfire horribly. Also, this isn't her fault. You can't control your emotions. Sometimes, they just become too strong, and they get totally out of your control. I know that, because that's exactly what happened with me and Ava. I thought I just wanted to sleep with her, but it's so much more. She's got me totally mesmerized...

Speaking of which, where has she gone off to? Did she even leave a message? I didn't have time to check my phone, but when I sort this out, that's the first thing I'll do.

Slowly, I release Ashley from my grip. She is shorter than Ava, somehow weaker, although they are of the same build. Brandon is right. Ashley's got that classical, timeless beauty, slightly enhanced, but we're not supposed to talk about it, even though it's pretty obvious to anyone with a pair of properly working eyes. Ava on the other hand, has so much more to offer. I figure, this is the exact worst time to mention any such thing.

"Are you OK?" I ask.

She looks down at her feet, refusing to let our eyes meet. "I just made a fool of myself again, didn't I?" She mumbles.

"No," I shake my head, grateful that we managed to diffuse the situation, which could have ended up explosively for both of us. "Sometimes, we let emotions get the better of us. But you can rest assured that I'll keep this between us."

"You will?" She looks up at me, her chestnut eyes trying to see right through me, as if whether to ascertain whether I'm telling the truth or not. This also isn't a lie. I have no plan or desire to talk about something so personal to anyone.

"You can count on that," I assure her. "Do you still want that coffee?"

I personally don't feel like having anything, but this came as a good distraction.

"I think I'll just leave, while I still have a little bit of my dignity left," she tells me, wetting her lips with her tongue, and wiping the corner of her eye. "Maybe, when I'm a bit better, we could have that coffee."

"I'd like that." I nod.

Slowly and cautiously, I lead her out of my bedroom, and towards the front door. She hesitates when I open the door, as if she's still considering staying. I hope that's not the case. But then, she turns around, and walks outside, without a single word. I listen to the sound of her footsteps until they disappear, and only then do I close my apartment door.

Fucking hell...

For the first time, I agree with the little voice. That was unexpected and an unpleasant beginning to my day. All the more so because I woke up to Ava gone from my bed.

I remember the phone, and I rush to get it. A few new emails, and there it is. A message from her. It's from eight am this morning.

I'm off to meet up with Sylvia. You were sleeping so soundly, I didn't have the heart to wake you up. You'll take me to that French bakery next time. I'm looking forward to going there with you. Also, I have an idea, and I need your help with it. Talk to you later.

I put my phone down, grinning. When you hear her talk and the way she acts, she presents herself to be so tough, and yet, when I help held her in my arms last night, she felt so small and defenseless, and that made me want to keep her safe from all the harm that might ever befall her. I don't think I've ever felt such a protective urge for someone. I want to keep her in my arms forever, to assure her that she would never know fear.

That barrier she has put up between us is slowly crumbling down. I can feel it. All I can think about right now is to absorb the hasty beating of her heart as she's lying in my arms. If I close my eyes, I could remember her head on my shoulder, how she would sigh occasionally as I held her close.

I head to the bathroom for a shower, although not even a cold shower would cool down the scorching need I have for her.

Chapter Fifteen

Ava

When I arrive at the café, I see that Sylvia is already there. Her bright pink hair is unmistakable, especially in contrast with her black clothes. She waves at me, and I approach her. She gets up to give me a hug, as we always do, and we both take a seat at the table.

I look around. It's still pretty early, but there are early birds like us, who wish to seize the day despite it being the weekend. Sylvia, however, isn't one of those people.

"You wanna tell me why we're meeting here instead of just meeting in our room?" She wonders.

The bright pink in her hair has lost its striking pink, and now is a bit washed out. Sylvia never pays too much attention to that. I notice she's not wearing a collar, and her nail polish is a bit chipped. That's how she usually is when she's happily in love: too busy to focus on her physical appearance. All she does is just focus on the guy she's with, and strangely, it works perfectly.

I sigh before I start. "I didn't want you to freak out if the police are still there."

"The police?" Her words echo, and I silently urge her to be more quietquieter. I don't want everyone here to know our business.

"Yes," I lower my tone, hoping she will do the same. "Last night, someone broke into our room."

"Are you serious!?" She gasps.

"I'm afraid so," I nod. "You didn't have anything valuable in there, did you?"

"No," her eyebrows raise at me. "Are you crazy? That's the first thing they tell you not to do. That and smoking. What about you?"

"No," I shake my head. "Nothing of value. I always take my stuff with me."

"Same," she agrees. "So, why the heck would someone break into the room of two poor college students? I mean, seriously? What were they trying to find?"

"I don't know," I admit. "But I bet it's not money or valuables."

Her face suddenly lights up, as if she remembered something. "It must have something to do with the letter!"

I don't know if I should get her involved in this mess. What if I'm putting her in danger, as well as myself and Gabriel? I know she wouldn't want to be left on the sidelines, no matter what. Besides, she's my best friend. Who will I share this with if not her?

"I spent the night at Gabriel's last night, and– "

"Wait, what?" Her eyes are about to pop out of their sockets, as she leans over closer to me. "Girl, do tell!"

"That's not what I was about to say," I smile, rolling my eyes playfully at her. "You're focusing on the wrong thing here."

"Na-ah, I'm focusing on the right thing here, and I sure want to– "

"Hi, what can I get you?"

We're both interrupted by the arrival of our waiter, and the moment I look up, I realize it's the waiter from the restaurant, where Gabriel and I went on our date.

"Hi, just a coffee for me, please," I smile.

"It's... you," he says, and I immediately notice Sylvia's eyebrows rising even higher.

"Me?" I wonder, not wanting to make this a big deal, but obviously he recognized me, just as I recognized him. "Yeah."

"From the restaurant?" He points at himself, and it feels a little awkward, but I decide to go with it.

"Yeah, of course," I nod. "I remember you. Didn't expect to see you here," I say it more as a joke, but from the tone of his voice I realize he took it as questioning of some sort.

"I, uhm, I work for both places," he nods. "You know, gotta make ends meet and all."

"Of course, I understand," I smile.

"So, uhm, that was your boyfriend I guess?"

The question catches me off guard. The thing is, Gabriel and I haven't really discussed our relationship, or maybe I should call it our situationship. It's obvious we both want more from this than a mere, occasional hookup, but it's hard to allow myself this. At least, on my part. I'm still afraid that he'll end up hurting me, and I don't want that. Love is hard.

Love?

No, that's not what I just thought. I meant, being in a relationship. Not love. Definitely not love.

"Yes, that was her boyfriend," Sylvia decides to jump in and help out. I smile appreciatively at her.

He turns to Sylvia, then back at me. "I thought so. A girl as beautiful as you couldn't possibly be single."

"That's very sweet of you to say," I smile at him.

People usually don't take kindly to others hitting on taken girls and guys, but he is so sweetly awkward, and I can't imagine him thinking any harm with this. After all, he just complimented me. Nothing else. He couldn't pose any real threat to someone like Gabriel, especially seeing that Gabriel is occupying every bit of space inside my heart. It's useless to deny it.

"Well, I hope he treats you well, as you deserve to be treated," he adds, with a slightly crooked smile, but that only seems to add to his endearing manner.

"Thank you, he does," I nod, at this point just wanting my coffee and to explain to Sylvia what I found out.

"Do you have apple pie?" Sylvia suddenly asks, and it feels as awkward as a bit of dust in your eye. You want it out, but you can't quite find it.

"Yes, we do," he nods, immediately turning professional. "It was freshly baked this morning."

"I'll have a piece then. Actually, make that two. And a coffee for her, thank you."

With those words, she signaled that his time was up. He got what he came for, and she just gave him his cue to leave. He smiled a little anxiously, then left.

I frowned at her. "That was a bit rude."

"He was hitting on you," she reminded me.

"He was being polite."

"Politely hitting on you doesn't make it any different," she reaffirmed, placing her hands on the table so that her bracelets jingled. "Now, we can finally talk about what really matters here. Gabriel."

"I wanted to tell you what we found out about the letter," I reminded her.

"OK, tell me, but then I wanna hear all about how you ended up at his place."

"Fine," I chuckle. "I don't know how you manage to always make me feel comfortable even when something unpleasant is happening."

"It's a gift, really," she curls her fingers, blows at them, then rubs them against her chest. We both burst out chuckling. "Now, tell me about that letter. What does the hopscotch song mean?"

"We still don't know that," I admit. "But we found out that our dads both attended this university."

"Aha," she nods. "Is that what your dad and his dad referred to?"

"Possibly," I shrug. "Like I said, we're still not sure what that means. Also, I have no idea what anyone could be looking for in our room. Maybe just to intimidate me, seeing that the letter didn't manage to do that?"

"Maybe," she admits. "So, you guys called the cops?"

"Clayton said we had to."

"The guard?"

"Yeah. The cops said it just could be someone from the dorm messing around, especially seeing that nothing was stolen. They actually seemed pissed that they were made to come out and check it out."

"Figure," she rolls her eyes. "All they want to do is scratch their junk while eating donuts, but God forbid they actually earn their paychecks."

Sylvia always hated cops. She told me about participating in some peaceful protest, and the cops just attacked them out of the blue. Ever since then, she's steered clear off of them and didn't want to have anything to do with the police in any shape or form.

"Well, in any case, they came and didn't really do anything. Just wrote a report and said to call them if we see something suspicious or if it happens again."

"Did you tell them about the letter?"

Actually, I had my own line of investigation opening open regarding that letter, and I didn't want to get the police involved, especially not after seeing them so enthusiastic about finding out who broke into our room. Sometimes, you are the only person who can help you. No one else. OK, maybe a hottie who seems to be involved in this as much as you are.

"No. Was I supposed to?" I play it cool, as if it's not bothering me anymore. Actually, it's not, exactly because I know what my next course of action is going to be.

"I don't know," she frowns, curling her fingers around her cup, and bringing it closer to her lips for a sip. "Maybe it was a good idea to mention it. What if the two are connected?"

At that moment, the waiter arrives, bringing two plates with apple pie and my coffee. For some reason, he's constantly staring at me, and I can't help but feel a little awkward realizing it. It's just not socially acceptable to stare at someone like that, so noticeably, yet it's equally socially unacceptable to point it out to someone and ask them, however nicely, to quit it.

"Here you go," he says. "Enjoy."

As soon as he disappears, Sylvia makes her comment. "God. I thought he's he was gonna sit down with us or something."

"Don't be so mean," I tell her, although there is no judgment in my voice. It's just who she is. She speaks her mind, and it's actually refreshing to hear. With her, it's what you see is what you get.

"So, is it safe to stay in our room now?" She wonders.

"Should be," I nod. "Clayton told me that he'll change the locks, and we should just pick up the keys on the way there now. It should be fine."

"OK, I'd hate to change our room," she admits. "I've gotten used to it."

"Me, too," I smile, taking a fork.

"What are you gonna do now?" She asks me that in a tone I've never heard in her voice. It's concern but mixed with more than just that. "Did you consider taking online classes maybe and going home for a while?"

"I can't believe you of all people are suggesting that," I confess. "I thought you were fearless."

"I am, but I didn't get that letter. I also didn't have someone follow me one night and then break into my room. Those are three very concerning things, Ava. It's one thing to be a tough guy, but another thing to recognize when your safety is in danger."

I never expected her to say something like this, and I know that she must mean it.

"I can't go home now," I tell her. "I'd have to explain why I'm doing it, and I don't want to worry my parents. Sylvia, I need to find out what this person wants."

"How?"

"Gabriel and I will check out some old record at the library," I tell her my plan. "From the time when both our dads attended university here. I'm hoping we'll find something that might shed some light on all this."

"Just…' promise me you'll stay safe, OK?"

"Promise," I smile. "How about we try this apple pie, which you forced me to have for breakfast."

"Nothing like some sugar to kick start your day," she winks at me, taking the first bite. "This is actually very good," she tells me with her mouth full.

I chuckle, taking a bite. She's right. Nothing like a little sugar to make you feel invincible.

Chapter Sixteen

Gabriel

I'm looking at a screen in a room that is almost complete dark. Ava is sitting next to me, her finger scrolling the mouse, which in turn is making the images flash before our eyes. I barely have enough time to skim through them, when she moves onto on to the next one.

"How many of these are there?" I wonder, as newspaper titles such as local football team scores, and milk prices drop significantly, appear before my eyes. None of that seems even remotely related to what we're looking for.

"You don't wanna know," she says, not even turning to me.

Her hair is puledpulled back in a loose ponytail, revealing her swanlike neck. Here, hidden in the darkness of the library, with us being the only ones present, I want to press my lips against the milky softness of her skin and take her right here, between the endless rows of books. I never thought that a library could be such an erotic place, but that is probably because I've never been with her before.

"But what exactly are we looking for?" I ask. "It would be easier if we knew that."

"Well, if I knew, I'd tell you," she says again, and this time also, her gaze remains focused on the screen before us.

A few more slides pass by, and then, she stops. Her eyes are focused on the screen, moving left and right rapidly as she reads. I do the same, skimming through the article about a dead student. A dead student who attended this same university.

She finishes reading the article way before me, then clicks a few options, and somewhere in the distance, a printer gets to work. She stands up and walks over to the other side of the room, waiting for the printer to finish. Then, she returns with the whole article in her hands.

"This might be it," she announces, dropping it right before me on a small desk.

She switches off the projector, and instead, turns on a little lamp to her right. Light immediately explodes all around us, and it takes my eyes a while to adjust to the new luminosity.

"Look," she presses her index finger to the first line. "K.D., a twenty-year old student is found dead after an initiation gone terribly wrong."

"Initiation?"

I keep reading, and then I see it. The name of the fraternity. It's the one my father was a member of. I look up at her, and I don't even need to ask her to know exactly what she is thinking.

"Was your father also..." My voice trails off, so she takes over.

"A member of Phi Omicron," she nods.

"Then, that must be where they know each other from," I confirm. "That must be the connection."

"But what about this guy here, K.D.?"

"You think our dads had something to do with it?" I ask, incredulous.

Sure, my dad can't be named dad of the year, but him being involved in the death of a student seems too farfetched, even for him. I'm sure she feels the same way about her father. Still, the article before us keeps taunting us. We came here to find answers, and instead, ended up with more questions than we had to begin with. Where do we go from here?

"It says it's just an initiation gone wrong," she explains. "The guy had asthma. They locked him up in a coffin, without his inhaler, and by the time they opened up the coffin the following morning, he was... dead."

The word dead feels like a hammer, breaking everything in its path. I wasn't expecting any deaths when I set out to discover this secret. I don't know what I expected, but it wasn't this.

"Was anyone blamed for that?" I wonder, but I think I already know the answer.

"The article doesn't say," she shakes her head, puling the papers closer to herself, as she kept reading and rereading the words before her. "Most probably they labeled it as an accident."

"An accident in which someone died, someone completely innocent," I conclude, trying not to imagine what kind of a death that must have been for that poor guy. Unable to breathe, closed up in a coffin. That's the real feeling of being buried alive, knowing no one would come for him no matter how loudly he shouted for help.

"That poor guy..." The words escape me.

She lifts her gaze to meet mine. There is compassion, sympathy, understanding, everything I ever wanted is in those eyes. I want her to always look at me like that.

"We need to find more info on this," she tells me.

"Maybe the police?"

"Not sure," she shakes her head. "Last time I had the pleasure of meeting a cop, they weren't very eager to help. We need to speak to our dads. That's the only way."

My memory is flooded with my father's reaction. Did he recognize her or her father? It's possible. Especially in light of this new evidence. They knew each other. That much was certain. They were also members of the same fraternity, the fraternity whose initiation rites ended up killing a student during the time that they were here. That had to be more than just a coincidence.

"Has your father ever spoken to you about Phi Omicron?" I ask.

"Not much," she says a little hesitant, as if she's trying her hardest to remember any possible conversations revealing this. "He just said it was a privilege to be a part of it, and that he, just like every other guy before him, passed the initiation. He didn't mention any coffins, though. What about yours?"

"More or less the same," I reply. "I think he has a framed photo of all of them in his office. I only asked once about it, and he just said they were all like brothers. They had each other's backs, no matter what."

"Even if that meant covering one another for an accidental murder?"

"I really don't want to believe that about my father," I say with a heavy burden upon my soul.

"Alright then," she concludes. "The first one we'll talk to will be my father. Come on."

She suddenly gets up, grabbing the papers and shoving them into her backpack. I don't follow her immediately, and she frowns at me.

"Why are you still sitting?" She wonders.

"We're going now?" I ask, all disbelieving. "It's nine pm."

"So?"

"By the time we get to your place, it'll be at least ten, right?" She nods. "We can't barge in this late."

"Then, you stay here, or in your apartment, if that's your choice."

She sounds a little hurt that I wouldn't follow her immediately. But that's not what I meant. I would follow her anywhere but barging in someone's home at this time of night won't be good for anyone.

"Let's do it tomorrow morning," I urge. "We're under the impression of everything we just read. Maybe it's not even related to what's happening to us. Maybe we're blowing this whole thing out of proportion."

"You won't make me change my mind," she replies calmly. "I told you. If you want to stay home, then stay home. I'm going to visit my parents, and I'll have a serious talk with my father."

"You think that he'll just spill everything after all these years just because you asked him to?" This turned out a bit more harshharsher than I expected it to, but luckily, she's too fervent about going to take it personally.

"I don't know if he'll spill the story, to use your expression, but I know I have to ask, right now. I won't be able to go to sleep or function. So, yes, I will do it now. Like, right now. As far as I can see, you have a choice. Come with me or stay behind."

With those words, she heads for the door, without even turning around to see whether I'm following her or not. Withing five minutes, we are sitting in my car, and she's directing my navigation where to go.

"First, we'll talk to my father," she tells me, as we're both focused on the dark road ahead of us. We pass traffic lights, which change colors, and I can't help but wonder whether that is exactly what's awaiting us, darkness illuminated by colors, which we need to make sense of. "Then, tomorrow morning, we'll talk to your father, and we'll get all the facts."

"Sure," I nod, my fingers clutching at the steering wheel. "And there isn't any doubt in your mind that this might not have anything to do with our dads?" I ask, and I'm not even sure what I'm expecting to receive as a reply. Whatever she says, I know it will be the truth. Her truth. That is all I ever wanted.

"I... I don't know," she admits, her voice thin and trembling.

Her mask has fallen. She isn't pretending to be strong and fearless any longer. She is just Ava, just her sweet, kind self, and not the image she has been projecting to the rest of the world. All I want to do right now is pull over and wrap my arms around her, telling her that everything will be alright whatever we find out after tonight.

"Then, we're going to find out," I tell her, smiling, only turning to the side to glance at her, then quickly returning my gaze to the road in front of us. "Together."

"Together," she smiles back, placing her hand on my knee. Her touch is scorching. It awakens my every sense. I still can't believe a girl has such an effect on me, even after we've slept together. Usually, the passions sizzles, but with her, it only seems to intensify every time I see her, every time I kiss her.

I remind myself that this isn't the time or place to think about that. We have other business to take care of, more important business.

During the trip, she falls asleep, just like the last time I drove her to my place. She sleeps like an angel, a few loose curls falling over her forehead and her closed eyes. Her lips are slightly parted, as if she wishes to speak, but keeps changing her mind in the last minute.

When we finally reach our destination, she remains asleep even when I stop the car. The house in front of us is small, cozy looking. It looks like its it's in desperate need of a paint job, but the old color is still holding up well. The windows resemble big, elongated eyes, peering into your very soul. All the lights are off.

"Ava?" I whisper to her, gently pressing my hand to her shoulder. She doesn't even stir. So, I shake her a little again. "Ava?"

"Yeah?" She mumbles, opening her eyes. It takes her only a moment to bring herself back to reality and to the present moment. Heaviness falls upon the soft features of her face, and she becomes gravely serious. "We're here." She echoes something we're both aware of.

"Yes," I nod, waiting for her to head out of the car.

She remains seated for a few moments longer, staring at the house.

"A part of me wants to go back," she admits. I know it takes a lot to admit that. "But I know I can't. I won't. We need to see this through." She turns to me and takes me by the hand. "Will you see it through with me?"

"Of course," I bring her hands to my lips, and I kiss them softly. "You can always count on me, always."

"Then, there is only one thing left to do..."

Chapter Seventeen

Ava

Maybe Gabriel was right. Maybe we should have come tomorrow, in daylight. Darkness seemed to enshroud our visit in ominous mystery, which ha sitshas its talons around my heart, clenching every time I inhale.

"Are you OK?" Gabriel asks, standing right by my side, as the key to my front door shakes in my trembling hand.

"Yes..." I nod.

Before I can say anything else, he gently takes the key from my hand and slide sit in, turning the lock and opening the door. Then, he moves to the side to allow me in.

"Mom? Dad?" I shout from the front door. There's something wrong about sneaking into your own house in the middle of the night. That's only OK if you are a teenager who snuck out, despite the warnings she's been given. I only did that a handful of times, and I didn't get caught once. This time, I am turning myself in.

Finally, the light turns on upstairs. I hear whispers, and my dad's face appears on the landing of the stairs.

"Ava?" He asks, completely shocked. "What are you doing here, sweetheart? Who's that with you?"

"I'm sorry to wake you up, dad, but I really need to talk to you about something," I say, finally entering my home, allowing Gabriel to close the door behind him.

My father descends the stairs, and immediately behind him, my mother does the same. She is wearing the same flowery robe she's had for years, the one she always wears the first thing when she wakes up and the last thing before retiring to bed.

"Darling?" Her voice is equally shocked as my dad's. "What's going on? You didn't mention you were coming, we would have stayed up to wait for you." She turns her attention to Gabriel. "I am Elizabeth, Ava's mother, but you can call me Lizzy, everyone does. And, this is Robert, my husband."

"I'm Gabriel," he smiles a little awkwardly. "Ava's... friend."

"Boyfriend?" My mother beams.

Gabriel turns to me, his eyes beckoning for help. "Yes," I reply instead of him, my heart leaping with joy at the smile of approval on his face.

"Well then, let's get your you kids settled, Robert, can you– "

"No, mom," I shake my head, taking my mother by the hand to prevent her from disappearing in the kitchen and starting to bake cookies or make coffee, which is what she always does when we have unexpected guests. "I want to talk to dad about something important. Very important."

"Sure thing, sweetheart," my dad nods. "What is it?"

"Let's sit in the living room," I suggest. "I think we'd all best be sitting for this one."

His forehead is now lined with worry, but he doesn't say anything. He just does as I suggested, and within seconds, we're all seated in the living room. My mother is awkwardly cracking her fingers, while my dad is waiting for me to start.

"I don't know where to start," I suddenly turn to Gabriel for help. He's seated next to me, and immediately takes my hand in his.

"A few things have happened over the course of last several days, maybe two weeks, which made us believe that they had something to do with you," he nods at Robert, "and my father."

Dad frowns. "I'm sorry, but I don't know who your father is."

"It's Reinier Price."

The silence in the room is palpable. All eyes are on my father, and he knows it. Despite that, he can't hide his shock, his complete and utter surprise at hearing that name. It immediately becomes obvious to everyone that he indeed did know Gabriel's father. It certainly sounds like a name that cannot be easily forgotten, especially if you had dark secrets connecting you with that person.

My father looks down at his slippered feet, burying his face into his hands. We expect him to talk, but there is only silence.

"Robert?" Mom is the first one to call out to him. "What's going on? Who is this man?"

Dad still doesn't reply. When he finally reveals his face again, he's slightly reddened.

"I didn't think you would ever find out," he tells me.

The weight of his words crushes me. He doesn't need to tell me anything else. He just confessed to everything that I'd been doubting, suspecting. At the same time, I've been hoping that all this is just a misunderstanding of epic proportions, and that I'd be returning back to the dorm with a heavy weight lifted off my back. It turns out it's exactly the opposite. The weight has just been doubled, and I'm not even sure I can hold it any longer.

"Find out what, Robert?" Once again, mother is the only one who can put her concern into words, which still sound as loving and tender as always. She always had the ability to do that. While others would remain silent and unable to speak, her voice brought back serenity into the room. Only this time, not even she had the power to restore peace. It was beyond her to do so.

"The initiation," Gabriel is the second to take over.

I still feel broken to my very soul, devastated that my deepest suspicions just came true. My father has been lying to me. He's not the person I thought he was. How could he have kept this secret from us all these years?

"What went wrong with the initiation?" Gabriel asks, and I'm grateful that he has the strength to go on with this. I doubt I have.

"Have you spoken with your father?" Dad asks.

"No," Gabriel shakes his head. "Tomorrow. Ava insisted we speak with you first."

"But... what brought you here? What happened?"

I listen to Gabriel tell my mother and father about someone following me, about the strange letter I received, about my dorm room being ransacked for something, although nothing noticeable was missing. My parents both listen intently, my mother's hand pressed to her lips in shock. I know she's wondering why I haven't told them any of this. I didn't want them to worry about me. I wanted to sort this out on my own. But it seems that our entire family is involved in this. Gabriel's as well.

"Someone wants you to know," my father whispers. "Lord knows I've carried this burden for far too long. I... I can't do it any longer. The truth needs to come out."

"What is the truth?" This question is torn from my chest, from my heart, from my very insides. This is the question only I have the right to ask.

"The truth is that no one is to blame," my father tells me. "And, when no one is to blame, then they call it an accident. But every accident happened as a result of several things gone wrong. That means that there are several people to blame. Only, that's not how the law works." He sighs heavily, raking is fingers through his hair. "Kellan Day. That was his name. I still remember his face as if I saw him yesterday. So... innocent and naïve. Just wanted to find a place to belong to. I was one of the elders at that point, and so was your father." He pauses a little to glance at Gabriel. "It was a new thing, the coffin. I always thought it was a bit too much. Ever since someone came up with the idea. But everyone just accepted it, and I had to go along with it. The idea was that the new pledges had to spend the night in a closed coffin, inside a basement of an abandoned house."

"That sounds... horribly frightening," I gasp.

"And it was," my dad confirms. "We had many pledges refuse to do it, saying it's too much. That was their choice, of course. But Kellan wouldn't quit. He and a few others accepted the challenge. We all thought it was... fun."

"Did you know he suffered from asthma?" Gabriel wondered.

"We were forced by the university to hand out these leaflets where pledges had to tick certain things, like their habits and health condition, especially if they had some rare illnesses or conditions that might require urgent medical care. But that was a double-edged sword. If they ticked any of that, odds were that they wouldn't be called back to join the fraternity. I... I didn't share this belief, but I had to stay quiet about it. The elders didn't want sick pledges."

"That's horrible," I gasp again. This is the side of my father I haven't seen. He's always been the one to speak up against any injustice. Knowing he didn't speak up when it mattered the most, crushed the image I had of him up to that moment.

"I guess that Kellan knew that, because I don't remember him ticking anything on his questionnaire. We actually considered him a very good candidate. He was smart, not very outgoing, but that wasn't crucial. We need a few clever students to raise our fraternity GPA, and we figured he was the perfect person for that. When he found out that he was to be put inside a coffin, I could see him turn pale. I asked if he wanted to back out, but he just shook his head at me. When the other elders were distracted, I whispered to him that he didn't need to do this if he didn't want to. He again shook his head. He assured me he was fine with it. I... I noticed the fear in his eyes, but I didn't understand it at that point. I thought he was just like the rest of us, a little squeamish about it being a coffin. Nothing else. I... I really wish I made him reconsider. If I only I said something, maybe he would have been alive right now."

"You gave him a choice," I remind him, although in a situation such as this one, such conviction matters little.

"He wanted to belong so much that he was willing to risk his own life for it. Eventually, that was exactly the price he paid."

"What happened when he assured you it was fine?" Gabriel asks.

My father turns to him with a steel gaze. "Your father closed the coffin lid."

I can see Gabriel now turning pale. Maybe he also believed that his father had nothing to do with it, or maybe that he was just an innocent bystander. That couldn't be. Not if he closed the lid, sealing the fate of that poor young man.

"The police ruled it an accident," my father concludes. "If Kellan didn't fail to write down that he had severe asthma, we wouldn't have put him inside. That was the way they presented it to the public, to the parents, to Kellan's parents, too. I remember not being able to look at them in the eye. I don't know if they blamed any of us. I know I would have, ifhave if I were in their shoes."

"But it's not your fault, dad," I tell him. "You can't read people's thoughts."

I want to make him feel better, but I know that's not up to me.

"I can't read someone's thoughts, but I can recognize fear when I see it. Kellan was afraid. I didn't know why. Now I do, but it's too late to change anything. Much too late." He sighs. "Maybe it's a good thing that you found out. I couldn't keep this a secret any longer. It was eating at my soul."

"Do you think maybe his parents are trying to punish us somehow, for the sins of our fathers?" I hear Gabriel ask. "Because, you could have made him change his mind, and my father was the one who closed the lid."

"No, I don't think so," my father shakes his head. "His mother died shortly after Kellan did. She was a sickly woman. They say that she just couldn't live anymore without her son."

"What about his father?" Gabriel wonders.

"He was much older than his mother, which would make him at least eighty now, unless he is also deceased. I honestly don't know," my father replies.

"Then, that leaves no one in his immediately family," Gabriel concludes.

"His brother," my dad adds suddenly. "Kellan had a younger brother. I remember him from the funeral."

"Could it be him doing all this, trying to intimidate us?" I interfere.

"Possibly," my dad nods. "But what is he trying to achieve?"

"Justice." Gabriel's words echo like a reminder of the people we ought to be. Righteous and moral, just and fair. I wonder if I'm all those things.

I see that this has taken quite a toll on my father, and we quickly say our goodbyes, with the promise that I'll come visit soon. I hug my father tightly on the porch to our little house, burying my face in his neck, just like I always did when I was a little kid and the world seemed to be too overwhelming and too scary. When I pull away, I see a tear glistening in his eyes.

"I'm sorry..." He tells me. "I'm sorry that I'm not the man you thought me to be."

I caress his cheek, and smile. "You are always the father I thought you to be."

With those words, I join Gabriel and we walk away from my home, wondering if things would ever feel the same again.

Chapter Eighteen

Gabriel

The drive back is silent, as we both expect it to be, I guess. Tonight has been overwhelming, to say the least. A part of me welcomes this silence because I can process things on my own, focusing on my own pain. But another part of me is focused only on Ava, her pain, her anguish, and all I want to do is make her talk until she gets it all out of her system and she is happy and cheerful again, as she always is, putting me in my place.

I occasionally glance at her, but all I see is her profile, illuminated by the passing headlights. She is staring at the road in front of her, just as I'm doing. I know she's devastated by what we just learned. I know, because I feel the same way.

Still, after a while, the silence feels oppressive. I need to hear her voice, to bring me back.

"Am I taking you back to my place?" I ask, not turning to her. A car passes us by, and its headlights almost make me blind.

"I don't know," she whispers. "I think... I'd like to be alone right now."

I immediately want to tell her that this is just an excuse. She won't be alone in her dorm room, either, because she has a roommate. The thought that she is pushing me away feels devastating, and worst of all, I don't know what to do about it. I can't make her want my presence. I can't force her to come to my place if she doesn't want to.

"Are you sure?" I ask. "Because, after a night like this, I want the exact opposite. I don't know how I'd handle being alone. Besides, I want us to go and talk to my father together."

She seems to have forgotten that we did only half of the plan. The second part was to go to my father's office and demand to speak to him about it. In all honesty, I have no idea how that will go. I've known my father all my life, but I've known him as a father and as a husband. I didn't know him as a student, a friend, and maybe even someone who had once been accused of causing someone's death. The thought makes me shudder. I never would have thought that I would find out something like that about my father, who always seemed like a decent man, a good person. Otherwise, I doubt my mother would have married him, if he showed her any lack in his character.

"Please?" I urge. "I really don't want to do this alone."

"I could just meet you in the morning or something," she replies, and I feel like I'm losing her. I feel as if this whole thing tore us apart, instead of bringing us together.

I sigh. "I understand you're scared." I have no idea where I'm going with this, but at least she's focused on my words, and she immediately flares up.

"I'm not scared," she almost scoffs. I don't hold it against her.

She's keeping that wall up again, and she thinks it's a good thing. She thinks that is the only way to prevent herself from getting hurt, while in fact, it's the exact opposite.

"What are you then?" I ask, and she immediately turns silent. She wasn't expecting that question.

"Nothing," she says vaguely. "I'm nothing."

"You can't be nothing."

"But that's exactly what I am," she continues. "I know you think I'm just saying it because I don't want to tell you how I truly feel, but that's not the case. I really feel nothing. I feel an emptiness inside, a disappointment. I didn't believe my dad was in any way involved in this until he admitted it himself. And now, I... I don't know what to think of him."

"That's easy," I tell her, my hands firmly placed on the steering wheel and my eyes fixated on the road ahead of us. "You think of him exactly what you thought up until now. He told you what happened. Did he do the right thing? No... not really. But we also can't be held responsible for other people's actions. Kellan should have considered his own medical health and he should have ticked that damn box. If he had, he would have been alive."

At that moment, the car behind us gets dangerously close, it's lights burning into our rear-view mirror. I look up, puzzled.

"What is he doing?" Ava wonders, looking back, but the lights are too bright. We can't even tell what make the car is, let alone something more detailed like who's driving.

"I don't know," I tell her, also confused, but not trying to make her more anxious. "Probably trying to overtake."

"Well, why doesn't he just overtake us then? There's no one else on the road but us."

As she's saying this, we notice that there is once again some distance between us and the car, but that is only for a moment, when whoever is driving that other car seems to step on the gas and rams us from behind. The entire car trembles under the pressure, and I try hard to steady the vehicle, keeping the speed higher than his.

"Gabriel?" Ava's voice trembles as she turns to me. "What's happening?"

"It'll be fine, Ava," I try to calm her down, but I'm barely managing to keep myself composed as well. "I think he's trying to run us off the road."

"Why?" She sounds scared now.

I don't want to tell her that I'd rather not find out. I step on the gas harder, hoping that we might either lose him or reach a gas station or something and stop there to look for help. For the time being, our safest bet is to keep moving as fast as we can. But the car behind us doesn't let go. He slams against us from behind one more time, almost making me swerve on the road, but I retain control of my car. Ava is silent at this point, but I see the way she's clenching at the side of the door, trying to keep herself in one place.

The car suddenly speeds up and comes to my left. I try to glance towards it, but the windows are tinted. It's impossible to see inside. I lower my window, shouting loudly at him.

"What are you doing, you idiot!?"

There is no reply from the other car, other than a straight hit to our side, and I feel us being dragged to the side of the road.

"Gabriel..." Ava musters, her eyes like two big suns shining in the darkness. "Do something..."

I have no time to think. I can't speed up any more than this, because I'm afraid that I'll lose control of my vehicle and we'll end up crashing. I guess that's exactly what this guy wants us to do.

Then, it hits me. I suddenly step on the break. The car tires screech against the road, and we come to a surprising halt. Luckily, we're both buckled up, so we remain safely in our seats. The car in front of us stops somewhere ahead, it's lights still on.

I don't do anything. Neither does the other driver. He revs a few times. I don't repeat his action. I want to see if he'll come back for us, or if he'll dare come out of the vehicle.

A few more seconds pass. We're all in complete darkness, save for the headlights of both our cars. Ava grabs my hand with hers desperately. I can feel all her fear in that tight grip.

"It'll be fine," I tell her, but right now, I'm still not sure if I'm saying it just for her or if I myself needed to hear that as well. In any case, it works. The reassurance loosens her grip, and it makes me focus harder on the car in front of us.

"What do we do now?" She whispers, as if she's afraid that the other guy can hear us.

"We wait," I nod, not taking my eyes off ofoff the other car. "We see what he's going to do next, and we react."

"Should I call the police?" She asks, but I shake my head.

"By the time they come, he'll be long gone," I tell her, sure of this scenario. "Just wait. It'll be over soon."

That is actually what I believe. It will be over soon. The only question is how it will end.

A few more dreadful seconds pass. I can hear our loud breathing, neither of us even trying to hide how scared we are. Then suddenly, the other car slowly starts to drive away. We wait a bit longer, just in case it decides to turn. Eventually, its taillights drift off somewhere in the darkness, and I finally turn to Ava.

"Are you OK?"

She inhales loudly, then exhales. "I think so. You?"

"Fine," I nod. "You sure you want to spend the night alone? After this?" She shakes her head at me fervently. "I'll drive you back to my place. We should be safe there."

"I really think we should call the police."

"And tell them what? That someone messed with us in the middle of the road?" I frown. "They'll think we're pulling a prank on them. They won't take it seriously, you know this."

"I guess you're right."

"Let's just sleep on this and go see my father first thing tomorrow morning. I know we already have almost the entire story figured out, but I want him to look me in the eye and tell me this. I need him to do this."

"I understand," she smiles, pressing her hand to my cheek. It feels scorching hot. "You don't have to explain anything to me."

I can't resist the urge to kiss her, so I bring my trebling lips to hers. She cups my face, pulling me closer. Our kiss is hungrier than ever, seasoned with fear and anxiety. But there is something deep down, underneath it all, holding us both together. I dare not say it out loud, although I feel it ringing on all bells.

When I finally pull away, we're both breathing heavily.

"Take me home," she says, and all I can do is obey.

Chapter Nineteen

Ava

I've never seen the inside of the Emerald Price building. I never had the reason to. Now, I was am in the elevator, riding up to the top floor, where the CEO himself had his office situated.

I look around the elevator and I can't stop staring. The blue is overwhelming.

"What?" Gabriel chuckles at me. "You've never seen the inside of a cylinder-shaped aquarium before?"

"This is... absolutely amazing!" I gush at the water around me, as we go throughout the core of this aquarium. "How did they make this?"

"Well, my dad loves the ocean," Gabriel shrugs. "As you can see. This aquarium boasts over two thousand different fish from 97 separate species. He very rarely has enough time to actually go and have a vacation by the ocean, so he figured he'd do the next best thing. He'd bring the ocean to him. That's why the last 82 feet of this elevator ride are basically an indoor aquarium."

I keep looking around at all the colorful fish peacefully swimming through the watery container. It almost makes you want to be a fish, too, just to see what it would feel like to swim through something like this.

"It must have cost a fortune," I gasp, imagining millions.

"Trust me, you don't want to know how much it cost," Gabriel frowns, and I can tell that he doesn't approve of that money being squandered on something like this. Of course, it's pretty, but it does nothing other than convince others of something they already know, and that is that Reinier Price is probably the richest man in the whole city. "For that amount of money, my dad could have fed ten African villages for a whole year, maybe more."

"But I've heard that your father is very generous when it comes to donations."

"He is," Gabriel nods, but something tells me that still isn't enough in the eyes of his son. "But I'm a believer in the old saying that you can always do more. And you can definitely spend your money much more wisely than building a freaking indoor aquarium."

I wonder what to say to that without sounding like I'm taking sides here. Everyone always expects from the rich to donate a part of their profits, but it seems that no matter how much they donate, there are always people out there who believe they could be doing more, donating more. Still, this feels like slippery grounds, and I don't want to discuss it with Gabriel, since he obviously doesn't take kindly to this huge aquarium being built here. The ding of the elevator saves the day. The doors open and we walk out into a long, endless seeming hallway with carpeted floors and paintings hanging off the walls. Gabriel walks first, and I follow him in silence. At the end of the hallway, there is a desk, with a large E and P in glittery gold plastered on the wall so huge it's impossible to miss.

Gabriel walks over to the desk, and the lady sitting at it. I remain a little behind him, wanting to give him some privacy as he speaks.

The woman immediately smiles at him upon seeing him, and I can't but feel a little jealous. Her green eyes beam at him, and she stands up, revealing a tall, lean model like body, wrapped up in a curve hugging dress the color of lilacs. Her body is flawless. Her hair is pinned up in a tight, severe bun, but it suits her cheek bones perfectly. Her makeup is bold, but still, you can't say it's too much. I wonder if that old stereotype is true that all CEOs of big companies have beautiful models as their secretaries or personal assistants. This here is another point for the stereotyped view.

"Mr. Price," she speaks melodiously to him, revealing a row of pearly whites, framed flawlessly by red lipstick that follows the line of her full lips to perfection.

"Theodora," he greets her back.

Even her name has that tinge of the exotic, and for a moment, I want to stand right next to him, and gently graze his hand, just to show that he's taken. Then, I remind myself I'm not a dog. I don't need to pee on him to show the world that territory has been marked. So, I remain put, but I don't fail to notice that she occasionally glances over at me, then back at him.

"Is my father in?" Gabriel asks, oblivious to the smiles that she is sending him, or perhaps he is just pretending for my sake. I choose to believe the first option. After all, if this is going to work, then we both need to trust each other. The notion is still frightening but thrilling at the same time. I want it, yet I'm afraid.

"Actually, he had an early meeting, and he failed to show up. I had to reschedule for tomorrow, but I tried calling him and– "

"Wait, wait," Gabriel lifts his hands to the level of his chest and shakes them left and right. "Did I hear that right? He failed to show up for a meeting? A business meeting?" Gabriel sounds more incredulous than I've ever heard him before.

"Yes," Theodora nods. "I tried calling him, but he's not picking up. After a while, it just sends me to voice mail. This has never happened before."

Gabriel just nods, then turns to me. "She's right. My father would never miss a meeting. He would rather allow a rabid dog to bite him and risk rabies, than miss a business meeting."

Under usually circumstances, I would find that funny. But now, it's just additionally worrisome.

"Does he have any other meetings today?" Gabriel turns back to Theodora.

"Yes," she confirms, glancing at her laptop, and dictating. "There is a meeting with Oregon Waterworks in an hour, and two more meetings with– "

"That's OK, thanks," Gabriel interrupts her. "I just wanted to check whether maybe he cleared his schedule or something."

"He didn't," Theodora echoes. "That's what has been worrying me all morning. He's never done this before, and you know I've been working for your father for ten years now."

I must admit, I wasn't expecting that. I figured old Mr. Price must be changing these pretty faces faster than he's changing his socks, but it turns out that she's a keeper, for whatever reason. I remind myself not to be so mean. It's just jealousy speaking, and I'm not used to the green-eyed monster taking control of my thoughts and actions. I need to cool it down.

"This is all very strange," Gabriel says more to himself than to either of the two women surrounding him. "When was the last time you saw him?"

"Last night," she replies. "I stayed until eight, eight thirty. I'm not sure exactly. I went in to ask him if he'll be needing me for the night, he told me no and I left him. When I came here this morning, I expected to find him already here, as usual. That didn't happen. I was surprised, but I thought maybe he worked late last night, and needed an extra hour of sleep."

"My father never needs an extra hour of sleep," Gabriel notes.

"Exactly," Theodora confirms. "I tried calling him several times. Like I said, after a while, it just sends me to voicemail. I've been meaning to call you, to ask what to do."

I watch Gabriel rake his fingers through his hair, turning around in the hallway. Then, he presses his hands to his hips.

"Cancel all his meetings for the rest of the day," he instructs her. "Make up a good excuse. He's at the hospital or something. I doubt anyone would believe any other excuse. Also, don't tell anyone about this, do you understand?" He continues, and she just nods obediently. "We don't want the press getting ahold of this before even we know what's going on and where he is."

"Of course, Mr. Price," she nods one final time. "You can count on me."

"OK, then. Let me know if you hear from him," he adds, turning to me and taking me by the hand, as we head back to the elevator.

Despite everything that's happening and all this confusion and mess, I can't help but be happy just to have him hold my hand like this. I wonder if this is what it feels like to be in love. Maybe. Maybe not. Maybe I'm still just mesmerized by everything that's happened between us, and maybe the magic will sizzle at some point. But until that moment, I will enjoy it.

I squeeze his hand back, as we wait for the elevator to come pick us up. He grabs his phone from his pocket and dials a number I can only guess is his father. He waits a few more moments, then hangs up.

"She was right," he sighs. "Rings a few times, then sends me to voicemail."

"That's a good sign."

"How?" He turns to me.

"He didn't turn off his phone," I point out. I'm guessing if something happened to him, his phone would be switched off."

"Unless he had a car crash or something..."

Mentioning the car crash makes us both remember what happened the previous night. The feeling of oncoming dread is still with me, although I try my best to keep it at bay and not acknowledge it. However, with Gabriel's father now gone missing, it's impossible not to think that something horrible might have happened.

"What would you like us to do now?" I ask him.

The elevator finally arrives, and the doors open, welcoming us in. I am once again washed over in the blueness of the water around us, and the bright colors of all the underwater animals I see around me. One little curious clown fish approaches me through the glass. I tap it, and it scatters away. I stare into the vast blueness wandering what it would feel it all that water engulfed us right here. Then, I start feeling sorry for the fish, who don't even know they're trapped inside a big tank. They aren't free. They just think they are.

Yet, they seem happy. The water is beautiful, crystal clear. They are well fed, well taken care of. They don't have a single care in the world. Their life is present and passing at the same time. It is always the same, yet they don't realize it. They are happy. We should be more like them. Less afraid. More accepting. More forgiving.

I turn to Gabriel. He seems lost in thought. I can only imagine how worried he must be about his father, not knowing where he is. Especially taking into account that his father has never done this before. What if something happened to him? That question keeps plaguing me, although I refuse to ask it out loud. Maybe Gabriel has already been asking that same question and is also preventing himself from speaking it out loud.

"I think we should go to his place," he finally tells me. "Maybe we'll find some answers there."

"Sure," I nod, squeezing his hand once again in agreement. "Whatever you want to do."

Suddenly, he turns to me. "How come it's you consoling me now, instead of the other way around?"

"I... I think I realize that we can't carry other people's burden on our back. Our own burden is more than heavy enough. Why take on the burden of others as well?"

He smiles, although it's a weak smile. Still, I appreciate it.

"I remember well what you told me about my father," I remind him. "I'm still torn that he didn't act the way I expected him to. I always thought he was the hero that this world needed, because that is what he had always been in my eyes, in the eyes of his little girl. But I've realized that he is also a human being, and as such, prone to mistakes. That doesn't make him any less of a good person."

"I said all that?" He grins. "Nice."

"Not in those words, but that was the message," I chuckle, forgetting all about the magic of the ocean around us and instead, focusing on the ocean that are his eyes. "Now, let's go over to your father's place and see what we can dig up there. No one can disappear just like that, off the face of the earth. There are always clues, and if we're careful enough, we'll find them."

He turns to me and wraps his arms around me. His cologne washes over me, heightening my every sense.

"How did I get so lucky to deserve a girl like you?" He beams at me.

"You refused to take no for an answer," I chuckle, kissing the tip of his nose.

The elevator door opens, and we step outside, into the world, ready for whatever answer it has in store for us.

Chapter Twenty

Gabriel

My dad's place is just on the outskirts of the city. He enjoyed being away from it all, the little time that he spent at home, but at the same time, he was still close enough to be able to reach any destination in the city within half an hour or so. The building complex is one of the most expensive ones in the city, and my father bought the whole top floor.

The doorman nods as I enter through the glass door. He is dressed in a perfectly crip suit, with a gold-colored name tag that says Phillip, just as you would expect a doorman to be named at a place like this. Not Chad or Tim or Nathan, but something royal like Phillip.

"Good evening, Mr. Price," he tells me, recognizing me.

I have been at my father's apartment a few times, though not that often, so Phillip must have taken a mental note to memorize me.

"Good evening, Phillip," I reply, stopping right next to him. "Have you seen my father today? Coming or going?"

Phillip tries to remember for a few moments, then shakes his head. His haircut is almost military underneath that hat, and his facial hair is non-existent, revealing a small, barely noticeable scar just to the left of his chin, resembling one of those childhood injuries that you never think of when they happen, but then they end up following you for the rest of your life.

"I'm afraid not," Phillip assures me. "Although I've been on duty since eight this morning. William had the night shift, so maybe you should ask him. You know yourself that Mr. Price has a tendency to come home pretty late and still head back to the office early in the morning."

"Yes," I agree. "That's true."

"Has anything happened?" Phillip obviously has a good eye for detecting human emotions written on people's faces, and I assume that the concern on both mine and Ava's faces is enough to reveal that something is off.

"I hope not," I press my lips tightly together. "It's just that my father failed to show up to work, and that is highly unusual for him."

"I know," Phillip is quick to nod. "I know him as a very conscientious businessman."

"So, I was hoping that I'd be able to come to his place and see if maybe he left some clue as to his whereabouts," I divulge my plan.

"Do you need to be let in?" Phillip asks cordially. In a moment like this, I appreciate the help he's offering, although I don't really need it.

"I have a key to his place," I explain. "I never expected I'd need to resort to it for something like this, though..."

"I can only imagine," Phillip tells me sympathetically. "I do hope that everything is alright. Mr. Price might seem strict and aloof on the surface, but I've spoken to him on a few occasions, and he's a good man, your father."

I honestly don't know how much of this is true. I doubt that my father has a habit of talking to the help in the places he visits or stays at, but still, it could be possible. In any case, I appreciate his words.

"Thank you," I reply, taking Ava by the hand and heading for the elevator. I press a button and we wait for it to come down.

"It seems like no one has seen your father since last night," she notices.

"Yes," I confirm.

"Do you think it's possible that he's traveled somewhere?" She wonders. "You know, maybe he has a girlfriend, a mistress, a lover, I don't know... I don't mean anything offensive by this. Just suggesting that maybe he decided to go somewhere with someone who suggested it to him, and just not let anyone know, even you."

I try to view it as a possibility, but it just doesn't ring true. None of it does.

"My father only loved my mother," I tell her. "They were high school sweethearts. I doubt he's even fucked anyone else in his entire life." I notice that I shocked her with my revelation. "I mean it as a good thing. He only had eyes for her. Even after she died, people... I mean, his friends, tried to set him up with different women, from very rich ones to somewhat poor ones, from the very beautiful to the much less so, and he always had the same answer to any of them. He was grateful for the chance, but no. I think he decided to mourn the loss of my mother for the rest of his life, and as weird as that may seem, I respect him more for it. That's why I think it's impossible for him to be having an affair of any sort, with a woman who managed to seduce him into going away for the weekend. I mean, it's preposterous!" I chuckle at the very thought, although I know Ava couldn't possibly understand that. She's never met my father or my mother to know the love that they felt for each other.

That's the kind of love I always wanted, but for some reason, I've been trying to avoid it for my entire life. Why? Because I've seen what it did to my father. My mother died, she left us too early. Her son was devastated. So was her husband. They knew her, they knew the warmth of her smile, the love in her gaze, only to be sentenced to a life without her.

I feared a life where I would give my all to someone, only for that someone to be taken away from me too soon. What would I be left with, other than pain and solitude? It was easier to just live a life of mindless fucking and nameless faces. But meeting Ava, I would never be able to return to that life. Even if she left me.

"I'm sorry, I really didn't mean anything by it," she suddenly says as the door to the elevator closes. "I just threw it out there as an idea."

"I know, and I'm grateful for it," I assure her. "I need objective input, because sometimes we think we know someone, but it turns out that they aren't what we thought them to be."

My mind immediately travels back to the mystery that we've been trying to solve and our fathers' involvement in it. Does his disappearance have anything to do with it?

We reach the top floor and I unlock the main door. When I open the door, I realize immediately that something's wrong. Ava walks in after me, and together, we're staring at the living room mess. The pillows are thrown all over the floor. The glass coffee table is completely destroyed, with little shards of glass scattered everywhere. We remain at a safe distance, unable to believe our own eyes.

"What happened here?" I hear Ava ask, although we could both come up with a few plausible explanations on the spot.

I don't reply. Instead, I rush over the kitchen. There is no mess there. It is in pristine condition, with a few still fresh-looking fruits in the fruit bowl on the kitchen island. From there, I go to the bedroom, and the same sight awaits me. The bed is nicely made, which means that he got up at some point in the morning, and made his bed, as he always did. He wouldn't be caught dead leaving his bed a mess. I remember this ever since the days we all lived together as one big happy family.

I walk over to the wardrobe and open it. His suits are hanging neatly from hangers, arranged according to color. I can't help but smile, then I immediately remember that I have no idea where he is or who he's with.

I rush back to the living room, the only room that has evidence of a crime. Ava suddenly walks over to a small pile of glass and kneels down next to it carefully.

"Watch out," I advise. "You don't want to cut yourself."

"Look," she points at something on the carpet, her index finger elongating in the direction of whatever it is she is showing me.

I lower myself to take a closer look. My face turns pale at the sight of blood. There isn't enough of it to consider it a lethal injury, but the thought of it being my father's blood makes my blood turn cold. All my fears are immediately triggered, because this isn't an imaginary threat. The bloody stain has just made it all too real, cemented in my mind.

I stand up and close my eyes. I want to close my mind as well, but that's impossible. It keeps showing me all these horrible images of what might have happened to my father, and the knowledge that I might not have either of my two parents sets in me.

"I think we need to contact the police," she tells me, and I know she's right. They'll know what to do, because I sure as hell don't know. I wouldn't know eve even where to start searching for my father. Do I even know him as well as I do?

"You're right," I agree. "I'll just... I'll call them from here and ask them to come right over. Can you stay with me?"

"Of course," she nods, placing her hand gently on my shoulder. "I'm not going anywhere."

Her presence means the world to me. I don't know how I'd go through this without her. I always thought that my father and I have grown apart, but that was because he was always there. He was always present to take the metaphorical blame for mother's death and him being away psychologically, choosing to focus on the death of his wife rather than the life of his son. I always resented him for this, although I could understand it, because I wanted her back as much as he did.

Now I realize that his presence in my life strengthened our bond again, almost invisibly. I didn't even know how much I cared about him until he went away, until he disappeared and is now nowhere to be found.

Suddenly, there is a knock on the door, and both Ava and I turn our gazes in that direction at the same time. I press my finger to my lips, silently wording shhh to her. She nods.

I tiptoe to the door, pressing my ear to the polished, wooden surface.

"Yes?" I call out.

"Mr. Price?" I immediately recognize Phillip's voice, so I open the door. He smiles a little awkwardly when he sees me, that scar on his chin even more visible contrasted against the light in the hallway. "This just arrived for you," he tells me, offering a pristine white envelope with absolutely nothing on it.

I take it, turning it around, looking for any proof that it indeed does belong to me. "How do you know it's for me?" I wonder.

"Because the man who delivered insisted it was of the utmost importance," Phillip explains. "He asked for you specifically."

"He asked for Mr. Price?" I ask, lifting my brow.

"No, he asked for Gabriel Price," Phillip clarifies. "I thought it was a bit strange for him to be delivering anything here to you, but he said he was informed of your presence here, and he was instructed to leave it for you immediately. He even wanted to leave me a tip, but as you know, we aren't allowed to accept tips."

"In that case, I'll make sure my father leaves you a nice Christmas bonus," I tell him, eager to open the envelope, but I don't want to do it with him here.

"Oh, no need to do that," Phillip smiles.

"I insist," I smile back. "Did you happen to take a good look at the man who delivered this envelope?"

"He was about five feet ten, with glasses."

"Sunglasses?"

"No, the ones for vision," Phillip explains. "He was wearing a dark grey hoodie and a pair of sweatpants of the same color. He seemed to be in a rush, urging me to accept the letter and assure him that I shall take it upstairs immediately. I suggested for him to do it himself, but he refused very firmly."

Maybe whoever delivered that letter knew what happened to my father. Still, from the way Phillip described him, the guy could have been anyone. Without any particular traits that set him apart from the rest of the world, I had nothing to go on.

"Thank you, Phillip," I nodded, leaning against the door, signaling that the conversation needs to be brought to an end. Phillip immediately takes the hint, and I'm even more adamant about getting him that Christmas bonus.

"If you need anything else, Mr. Price, I'm just a call away," he nods quickly, then closes the door himself.

I listen to the sound of the self-locking doorknob, and I walk back to the living room, holding the envelope in my hands. She has the same concerned look on her face as me. I open the letter, almost dropping it, so I grip it even more tightly. I unfold the letter. Then, I read it out loud.

"No police. Abandoned warehouse on the corner of Weston and Third. Nine pm today."

"Oh my God..." She gasps, pressing her hand to her lips, with only her eyes revealing shock and disbelief. "Your father is kidnaped."

Chapter Twenty-One

Ava

"I don't care what you say, Gabriel, I'm not staying in the car," I finalize our argument which started the moment we headed for our rendezvous point.

At first, he thought he could leave me at his apartment. I understand he's worried about me, and he feels like he'll need to watch out for me as well, while we're there. But I want to be there for him. I want to be a part of this, and I know I can help. Especially knowing that we didn't contact the police, because the note warned us against it. That was actually a good sign. That meant his father was still alive.

"There's no reasoning with you," he sighs, finding a parking spot several streets down, so we'd need to walk there unnoticed.

"I'm not bailing on you now when the going's getting tough," I explain.

"I'm not saying you are, Ava. I just don't want something to happen to you," he admits. "I... I wouldn't forgive myself."

"Think of it this way," I take him by the hand, his face illuminated by the streetlights above us. "I'll be close to you, so you'll be able to save me, if I need saving. If you make me stay in the car, I might need your help and you won't be here."

He thinks about it for a moment, then snickers. "You're a smartass, you know that?"

"Of course, I do," I nod, and he quickly brings my hand to his lips, giving my palm a kiss.

"Just promise me you'll be careful, OK?" He finally agrees, because he knows he can't make me stay behind.

"Only if you promise me the same," I curl all my fingers at him, except for my pinkie. He grabs it with his pinkie fingers, then shakes it.

We get out of the car and start walking down the street. We're both wearing dark hoodies over our heads, lowered over our foreheads.

Gabriel is rushing, and I'm trying to keep up. The tension around us is palpable. A part of me wishes we got the police involved. They could have followed us somehow, unbeknownst to the guy we're about to meet. This way, we're doing it on our own. If something happens to us, no one will know where we were or what we were doing. I dread to even consider that possibility, so I try not to think about it.

When we finally reach the warehouse, he urges me to stay behind the corner of the nearest house. This way, we're out of sight. The warehouse is bathed in darkness. The only streetlight that is there isn't working.

"Where is the entrance?" I ask, looking around us, trying to make sense of the area, but it's hard when you've never been here.

"I checked online," he whispers. "It should be right in front of us."

"Is that where we're supposed to go?" I wonder, as fear slowly joins me on this journey.

"He didn't specify," he reminds me. "So, I figured, we'll just barge in through the front door."

"What if there are more people there?"

"Don't worry," he pats his pocket. "I brought a little friend."

He lifts his hoodie to reveal the silvery gleam of a small gun.

"Where did you get that!?" I gasp for air.

"Shhh," he reminds me. "You don't want to announce to the guy we're here, do you?"

"Sorry," I whisper.

I don't tell him that I wasn't expecting him to carry a gun with him, but on second thought, that doesn't seem like a bad idea at all. It's just the two of us, and I'm a girl. We're totally outnumbered if there are more people, or if they are armed. This way, we just might have the upper hand.

"It's my dad's," he explains, hiding the gun from plain sight. "I took it from his study."

I don't ask how he even knew it was there. All I know is that I'm glad we're not going into this with only our knuckles.

"You ready?" He asks, and all I can do is nod.

The truth is I have no idea if I'm ready for anything that is about to take place tonight, but I know that I am ready to go through it with him. We sneak across the street, and over a wired fence. We creep past the main building then hide behind a big dumpster, which smelled worse than a junkyard.

"There's the entrance," Gabriel tells me. "Are you sure you don't want to stay here?"

"Can you stop asking me that?" I frown. "It's difficult to argue while whispering."

He nods, and even in the darkness, I can tell he's smiling. He heads first, and I rush after him. I'm listening to every possible sound around us, or behind us. But there is nothing. This whole place feels deceptively deserted, and I know that we can't be lulled into that sensation of thinking that we're alone here. Because we're not. It's just a matter of finding the right location, the one we've been invited to.

Gabriel slips through the open door of the largest building, and I do the same. It feels like someone turned off all the lights. The floor underneath me is hard. I spread my arms wide around me, blindly feeling for Gabriel, unable to speak. I mustn't speak. I have to find him without calling out to him.

All of a sudden, someone pats me on the shoulder.

"Shhh, it's me," he whispers as softly as he can, but even his presence is unable to soothe the wild beating of my heart.

I'm wondering what are we are even doing here all alone. Did we just willingly enter into a trap? I can't help but feel ensnared somehow. A part of me just wants to turn around and rush out the way we came in, but I force myself to stay put. I need to be brave for myself, for Gabriel, for both of us.

"There," he mumbles underneath his breath, and we both see a faint light at the far end of the room.

I walk slowly, without his hand on my shoulder. It's harder to keep balance in the darkness. I never thought blind people had that to deal with, too. I stumble onto a pile of cardboard boxes, but I manage to stop before any of them fall down onto the ground, making noise. I stop moving for a moment. So does Gabriel. We listen to see if anyone would appear, or if there are any signs of danger. Nothing.

We keep going towards the light and it takes us to another, smaller room. There is a large curtain, dividing the room in two. A shadow looms from behind the curtain. I stop behind Gabriel, and he extends his arm towards me, in a subconscious effort to keep me safe.

I swallow heavily waiting to see if someone will jump out from that curtain and lunge right at us, but nothing happens. The dark, shadowy figure remains motionless.

Gabriel looks at me, and gestures that he will go take a look, but I need to stay where I am. This time, I nod.

The room is empty, devoid of any objects, apart from that light blue curtain. The fabric isn't completely see-through. It's more of a shower curtain, allowing you to see just faint outlines of what's happening behind.

Gabriel starts for the curtain slowly, one foot ahead of each other. His hoodie is slightly lifted, revealing his gun, which is still not in his hand, but it could probably be in less than a second. I look down at his feet, and I gasp.

He stops. Fist he looks at me, then he glances over where I'm looking. There is a small pool of blood right in front of him. The blood looks caked. So, whatever happened here, didn't happen in the las last several hours.

Gabriel nods at me, then continues towards the curtain. Tension grips at my very neck, making it increasingly more difficult to breathe. My whole body is trembling with fear, with anticipation, with the desire to run away, but my legs have turned to ice, freezing me in position. Also, I could never run away and leave Gabriel all alone here, not after I promised I would be by his side no matter what. I realize that, despite all the fear, I truly meant it.

He finally reaches the curtain. I watch his fingers piercing through the air, diminishing the distance between them and the curtain which is hiding whatever is behind. I can only imagine the fear he is feeling right now. Yet, he pushes through it.

He pulls the curtain in one effortless swoosh, and the curtain flies all the way to the other side, as it's hanging on a rod from the ceiling. I gasp noiselessly upon seeing that there is a man sitting on a chair. The second thing I notice is the rope tied around his body, making it united with the chair. The rope starts from his neck, slithers around his shoulders, upper and lower abdomen, only to tie both his legs separately to the legs of the chair. There was no getting out of those ropes on his own.

"Dad!" Gabriel shouts, despite all our initial efforts to remain quiet.

We arrived a little early, hoping for a surprise effect. It turns out that the joke was on us, because it was us who were the surprised ones.

Gabriel drops down to his knees, his gun disappearing from sight. He is trying to loosen the ropes that have his father bound, but he can't do it. They are too tight.

His father's head rests limply forward, all his hair falling right over his forehead and his eyes. His shirt sleeves are rolled up, and I notice blood stains on what was once probably a pristine white business shirt.

"Dad?" Gabriel cups his father's face with his hands, lifting it towards him, but the man is unresponsive.

"Check his pulse," I urge, finally mustering the courage to walk over to him.

"Where?" Gabriel asks, frantically.

I'm sure he knows exactly in which places on the body he should check for a pulse, but he's under too much strain now to think rationally. I lower myself next to him.

"Keep his head straight," I instruct, pressing my index and middle finger right underneath the man's jaw, to the side of his neck. It's barely there, but I feel it. "He's alive."

"Oh, thank God..." Gabriel sighs heavily. "We have to get him out of these ropes."

What we need now is a knife, yet neither of us even considered bringing it here. He lets go of his father's face, and it slumps down onto his own chest once more, but not before I notice the swollen eye and the cracked lip. I'm sure he put up a fight. There was proof of it in his apartment.

"Maybe if we find something here, we might be able to– " Gabriel starts, but he's not allowed to finish, as a figure emerges from the darkness of the hallway we first passed through.

"Isn't that endearing?" The tone is mocking us. "One big happy family. I'm truly happy for you, even though it was you who ruined mine."

We both turn around, and I realize I've seen him before.

Chapter Twenty-Two

Gabriel

It's him. It's that weird waiter from the restaurant.

He's standing in the doorway, blocking our exit. There's barely enough light to see him properly, and the shadows hit him from behind, making him appear twice as big as he is. In fact, he resembles more a monster than a man, which is exactly what he has become for us both in the past several weeks. Now that we're finally face to face, I don't know whether to feel afraid, relieved or angry.

I immediately inspect his hands. He doesn't seem to have anything in them, but I can't rule out the fact that he might be armed, just like me. Any man who's willing to undertake such a crazy endeavor can't be in his right mind. And any man not in his right mind is twice as dangerous as a normal man, because you can't possibly predict his actions, because you have absolutely no idea what he's thinking or planning next.

"You're Kellan's brother, right?" I start, feeling my lips dry out with every word I say.

I keep an eye out on his actions, but he seems calm and composed, much more so than either of us. Ava is standing next to me, and my father is still sitting unconscious on the chair. It's a strange get together, one I suppose this man has been planning all along. I wonder if this is how he imagined it.

"You didn't even bother to learn my name?" The guy chuckles, scratching the back of his neck. It seems like he's having fun. Maybe he's even crazier than I thought him to be. "Do either of your fathers know it?"

His voice echoes, cutting through the thick silence that has been oppressing us until this moment.

"I don't know," I reply before Ava has the chance to. I don't want her to say anything. Knowing the sharpness of her tongue, she might piss him off, and aim all of his anger on herself. I need it focused on me. Only me. That way, I can assure that she might leave this mess unharmed. "You kidnaped my father before I could even talk to him about any of this."

"What about yours, Ava?" He turns to her.

Kellan's brother. That's what he referred to him. We both know it.

"Why are you doing this to us?" I demand to know, realizing that my best strategy is to attack, and not dive into his story, which he'll surely want to share with us. I need to make him edgy, nervous. When people are nervous, they lose focus. And when they lose focus, you can defeat them. "Neither me nor Ava have anything to do with this."

"Of course, you do," he corrects me. "And it's Kendrick, by the way."

I remember the tone of his voice at the restaurant. He was apologetic, apprehensive, shy. The man standing before us now is the complete opposite. His brows are furrowed, bushy, like two caterpillars just above his eyes. His Roman nose is protruding from his face, and he's got palms the size of shovels. He's wearing loose fitting clothes, but from a quick glance, I'd say he's in pretty good shape. Taking him on won't be an easy task. But if it's only him, and if he's unarmed, we're good. I just need to calculate my steps, so no one gets hurt. Hell, I don't even want him to get hurt.

"Listen, Kendrick," I tell him, lifting my hands slightly up in the air, so he can tell I'm also not holding anything. "I understand you're pissed. Hell, I'd be, too, if I were you."

"Would you now?" One bushy caterpillar jumps up slightly higher than the other. "Tell me about it, then,"

"Your brother's death was ruled an accident," I remind him. "I know that's unfair. That's fucking unfair, but he didn't state his medical condition anywhere. He chose not to."

He doesn't say anything. Instead, I notice his jaw tensing, as his teeth are grinding against each other. He's losing his cool. I also know this is a dangerous path I'm treading, but I need him to get pissed. I need him to act first, so we can react.

"Are you saying this is my brother's fault?" He growls at me loudly.

"No, no," I shake my head quickly, and my hands as well, to strengthen my refusal of this idea. "I'm saying it's no one's fault. It was just a sequence of horrible decisions which unfortunate ended in a tragedy. Listen, I know what it is like to lose a family member..."

His jaw relaxes. He's listening.

"My mother died, and I was angry at the world. Even at him," I turn around, pointing at my father. "That man there is many things. He's been a lousy father. He's been a ruthless employer. I doubt he's a very good friend, too. But I know one thing and that is that's he's not a murderer."

Kendrick seems to ponder it for a moment, then his eyes flare up with newfound hatred. "Your fathers are the reason I don't have a family anymore. I was just a kid, when my mother told me that my big brother won't come home ever again. Do you know what that does to a kid??"

I notice Ava trembling. I walk over to her and wrap my arms around her shoulder. Kendrick barely even notices it.

"Then, just a few years later, she dies, too. She dies of a broken heart. She dies because her mind told her body to shut down because she didn't want to live without her son anymore!"

He turns around and finds a small cardboard box to the right of him, kicking it all the way to the opposite wall.

"All I've ever heard from my father was Kellan this, Kellan that. If he were here, he'd do everything better than me. But you know what he can't do? He can't bring the ones responsible for his death to justice. Only I can do that."

"Kendrick..." Ava's tender voice fills the room around us. "You can hurt us. That is your choice. But that won't bring Kellan back. In fact, that won't do anything. It will just make you feel even worse."

"Kendrick, buddy... let's end this before any of us got hurt," I add, taking a step to him, but before I can say anything else, he reaches back and gets out a gun. It's pointed straight at us. I immediately stand in front of Ava, shielding her with my body.

"Don't you fucking dare call me buddy!" Kendrick's hand is trembling, with the gun in it. Right now, him being nervous and edgy doesn't work in our favor. It might make him trigger happy. We need him back to his calm and composed self again.

"You're right, you're right," I try to mirror Ava's tender voice, but it's hard. She does it so effortlessly while mine feels too forced. The last thing we need right now is make him even more edgy. "It was just a figure of speech. I apologize, I didn't mean anything by it."

Kendrick hits his temple with the handle of the gun several times quickly.

"Fuck! Fuck..." He mumbles more to himself than to us. I don't know what his plan was, but it obviously wasn't going well... for any of us.

"You..." The gun is back, pointing straight for us, "you all need to pay for what you've done!"

"We haven't done anything," Ava reminds him. "Neither have you... yet. The choice is still yours, Kendrick. Everything is under your control. Everything. The choice that you make now will follow us all until the end of our lives. You'd better make it a good one."

I'm not sure if it's a good idea to lay a guilt trip on someone pointing a gun at us, but the way she's saying it almost feels loving. She isn't judging him. She is merely telling him the way things are in a way that he is allowing himself to hear.

"I can't... I can't..." He shakes his head so quickly I can barely follow the motion with my eyes. The gun in his hand dips a little, but he pulls it up again even more quickly. "We're here now. I need to see this til till the end. I must."

"What will your father think? If you hurt any of us, you'll to prison for a long time." I warn him, but it's something he's aware of. "Your father won't have anyone left. He only has you."

"Why do you think I'm doing this, huh!?" He hisses loudly, spitting along the way. "All he's ever done is compare me to Kellan! I've never been good enough, never! But now, if I avenge Kellan's death, maybe my father will see that I'm as good as my brother, maybe even better!"

"And Kellan?" Ava suddenly comes up with another strategy. "I've heard that he was a good person. The kind that would never even hurt a fly. He was shy. Helpful. Overall, a nice guy you'd want by your side through thick and thin. I understand your conflicting feelings about your father. It's not easy being compared to someone you can never outdo because they're not around anymore. But... what would Kellan think if h he saw you pointing that gun at us right now?"

If I could, I'd clap for her. This was perfect. The confusion on Kendrick's face is palpable. She managed to get to him. The way wasn't through the father, because the father was obviously at the root of all this, without even knowing, feeding his son's mania for years. The way through to him was through his brother.

"You're just trying to confuse me," he snarls suddenly. "Because you know you are to blame, all of you. You are no less innocent than your fathers..."

It sounds like that's the end. I close my eyes, knowing that if he shoots, the first bullet is mine. Hopefully, he doesn't have more. Or he empties them all at me.

"No..." I suddenly hear the weak voice of my father.

We all turn to him. He's managed to lift his head. There is a dried trickle of blood in the corner of his lips. I've never seen him like this. If I didn't know any better, I wouldn't even know him. His eye is so swollen that half of his face is barely recognizable. His cracked lip is making his speech slurred, but he's trying his best to talk.

"They aren't... to blame... for anything..." My father says, when a bout of violent cough attacks him. Is His entire body is shaking from the onslaught.

I head over to him, but I'm warned against it.

"Stay where you are," Kendrick orders. "Nobody movemoves!"

"I just want to untie him, he'll drown in his own blood!" I shout angrily, not caring even if he does pull that trigger. I know that my father is coughing up blood and his breathing is short and ragged.

At that moment, the gun fires.

Chapter Twenty-Three

Ava

I hear the gun go off, and I immediately think it's Gabriel. My eyes are frantically going over every inch of his body, looking for the slightest indication of him being shot. There is no blood on him. He is still standing. That is enough to assure me that he's unharmed. I lower my gaze to my own body then, thinking perhaps the shot missed him, but it hit me instead. I feel no pain, other than the dull ache inside my mind, which is growing by the minute. My body is also intact.

It is then that I realize there is a pool of blood on the white shirt of Gabriel's father. The shot hit him in the abdomen. I run to him, taking off my hoodie, and pressing the wound, hoping to stop the bleeding. My whole body is shaking, as if there is an inner earthquake and nothing I could do would pacify it. Gabriel's father coughs some blood, then gurgles something at me.

At that moment, I hear another gun shot, and I think to myself it's all over. The second shot must have hit either Gabriel or me. I'm just in such an adrenaline shock that I can't feel the pain. That must be it.

"Just hang in there..." I tell the man in front of me, feeling my hoodie soaking up all the blood.

Somewhere behind me, a body slumps to the floor.

"Gabriel!" I scream, turning around.

A million images pass through my mind, gnarly, announcing a bleak future without him in it. My brain ceases to function in that single second which threatens to freeze me for eternity. I imagine my life without Gabriel, and I don't like a single aspect of it. Even if we had just these few weeks between us, I realize that I wouldn't change them for anything else in the whole world. I can't keep pushing everyone away just because I'm afraid of getting hurt. Risking it all is what life is all about, because you might be risking the loss of everything you've ever known, but at the same time, you might be gaining so much more than you ever hoped you'd get.

I see his body breathing heavily, his fingers trembling, holding the gun. But... he's standing. It's not him who's lying on the floor, in a pool of blood.

Gabriel is pale. His mouth is agape at what he's done. Disgusted, he throws away the gun, and rushes over to us. He cups my face quickly, frantically.

"Are you OK? Are you shot?" He is speaking quickly, swallowing half of the letters.

"I'm fine," I nod, turning to his father. I don't need to say anything, because he sees that my hoodie is completely soaked with blood now. I press my fingers to the man's neck. I can barely feel a pulse. It's even weaker now than it was before.

"Dad!" Gabriel drops down to his knees, and his father lifts his gaze. Pain is immediately etched on his deformed face, but he still tries to open his eye to look at his son, what might be for the last time.

"Gabe..." He tries, but instead of more words, only air comes out of his mouth.

"No, shhh... don't try to speak," Gabriel is desperate. "We need to call the ambulance."

"Press here," I urge him. "Don't let go."

"I w-won't," his voice is on the verge of breaking.

I stand up, grabbing my phone from my pocket and dialing 911. The call only takes me a minute, and I'm assured that both the police and the ambulance are on their way.

I turn to look at Kendrick. I walk over to him and notice that he's still holding the gun in his hand, although he's not moving. I lower myself to the ground to take his gun, just in case. I've seen too man many bad movies to know that the bad guy always comes back for one final scare, and the protagonists need to be ready. I never thought

Gabriel and I together would be the protagonists of our own movie, but here we are, bloody but still alive.

I take the gun from Kendrick's hand, his fingers still clutching at the handle. He is lying face down. I can't hephelp but feel saddened at the way his life ended. He didn't deserve this. Neither did his brother or his mother. When a family is marred by tragedy, all the members of that same family are equally affected, no matter who the one physically hurt is. Everyone hurts mentally.

Just as I'm about to stand up, Kendrick's hand grabs me, his fingers digging into my wrist. I jump back, but his grip is too tight. He just won't let go. Just one of his eyes opens up, staring at me. Then, I see it. It's not malice. It's sadness. It's regret. Emotions all too well known to the human race. A small, barely noticeable tear rolls down his face.

"I... I'm sorry..." He manages to whisper before he finally releases his hold of me forever.

Still trembling, I stand up, watching him, my gaze burning into the back of his skull, half-expecting him to get up again. Only this time, he doesn't. He's gone off to a better place, where hopefully, he will meet up with his brother and his mother. I can only hope that they'll forgive him for what he tried to do.

I rush back to Gabriel, who is still pressing on his father's wound.

"The ambulance is on its way," I tell him, not really knowing what else to say.

"I just hope it won't be too late," Gabriel replies, not taking his eyes off his father, who once again tries to lift his head and use the last remnants of his strength to address his son.

"I know..." The man speaks in a torn way, as if every word is pulling his every muscle out of his body raw. "I haven't been... the best father..."

"No, dammit, shut up and save your strength!" Gabriel pleads, his voice on the verge of breaking.

"Just know that... I love you..."

With those words, his head bobbed down once more, but this time, I'm not sure he would be lifting it again. I press my fingers to his neck.

"He's still alive!" I exclaim, triumphantly. "Just keep talking to him, OK? He mustn't fall asleep."

"Dad, dad," Gabriel does as I told him. I take over the pressure on the wound, and he uses both his hands to lift his father's head and steadies it. "Remember that picnic on Lake Willow? That little lake mom discovered, and when she made us walk for three hours to get there? Remember?"

I look at the now featureless face of his father. I don't expect a response. Maybe he's already decided to let go, and no one could blame him. We don't know the pain he's in. But then, I see it. There is a faint movement of his lips, as if he's trying to smile. One eye opens only slightly, focusing on Gabriel.

"Yes, dad... remember? Remember how mom used to laugh at corny jokes? The cornier the better? What was that last one she told, and kept retelling?"

"One..." His father suddenly speaks.

"... with everything," Gabriel finishes his father's thought, unable to hide his smile. "That stupid make me one with everything joke, remember?"

His father mumbles something in reply.

"How did it go?" Gabriel thinks about it for a moment, then continues. "How does the Dalai Lama order pizza? He says make me one with everything!"

I can't help but chuckle. That really is one of the corniest jokes I've ever heard, but Gabriel and his father are both still here. His father's eye is open. He's fighting with his last breath to stay here, with us.

"She loved that joke," Gabriel remembers. "Especially when people didn't get it. She was so shocked when they didn't get the reference."

"She... so... sweet..." His father replies, with every second word trailing off soundlessly.

"She really was," Gabriel agrees.

At that moment, we heard the distant sound of the ambulance approaching.

"Do you hear that? They're here! Just hold on for a little while longer, can you do that?" I hear Gabriel plead.

A minute later, a group of people barge in. The police are first, followed by the EMT's, who immediately rush over to us.

"We'll take it from here," a guy says, and we both step aside.

We watch as they lower Gabriel's father onto a stretcher, checking the wound. They put an oxygen mask on his face, securing the airway. Secondly, they use pressure bandages, the cervical collar and off they go, heading out.

"Do you need help?" A young EMT comes to ask us. "I've already checked him." She gestures as Kendrick. "Unfortunately, he is beyond help."

"We're good, thanks," I tell them, and Gabriel just nods.

"Which hospital are you taking him to?" He asks. "I need to be there when my father wakes up."

"We can take them both to the hospital, after we ask them a few questions," a police officer suddenly pops up between us, with a notepad and a pencil in his hand. Another appears right next to him. The EMT just nods, then leaves us.

I'm too exhausted to think straight. All I want is to go to the hospital and make sure that Gabriel's father is alright. But I understand the need to question what happened here. After all, someone died. Once again, it's an accident. But who will be to blame this time?

"Do you mind telling us how you ended up here in the first place?" The first police officer asks, ready to take down as many notes as he can. I appreciate his enthusiasm, and the obvious desire to sort out this mystery.

"I guess you want to hear it from the start," Gabriel inhales deeply, then begins with our story.

Chapter Twenty-Four

Gabriel

We spent the night in the hospital waiting room, for the sole reason that we refused to leave. They brought my father straight into surgery, and when it was finished two hours later, they informed us that he needed to sleep it off for at least a few hours, as he still wasn't out of the woods, but we were lucky because the bullet missed all vital organs. When he wakes up, we'll be allowed to see him only for a few minutes.

I open my eyes with a horribly stiff neck. I rub the back of my head as I sit up on the chair in the waiting room, but it helps little. I glance over at Ava. She is sleeping on the opposite row of chairs, and she looks quite comfortable doing so.

The first rays of the morning sun are visible through the numerous windows. Ava stirs in her sleep, wrapping herself up even more under the blanket that a kind nurse offered us both. That means we've been here entire night. Maybe my father has regained consciousness.

I rub my eyes, as I stand up, heading for the nearest coffee machine. It's just colored water and tastes like that as well, but I need to focus my mind on something while I'm waiting for a nurse to pass by so I can ask her about my father's condition.

I dig into my trouser pocket for some change, then slide a few coins into the slot. I press the button for double espresso. Hopefully, it'll be better than the Americano they're known to serve in hospital cafeterias. I focus on the whirring sound of the machine, then a thin stream of dark water drips right into a white paper cup. When I bring it to my lips, I have to admit that it doesn't smell half bad. It's either that, or I'm too tired to care about the taste of what I put in my mouth. Whatever the reason is, I blow into the cup, then take a little sip.

"Is it any good?" I hear a voice behind me.

I expect to hear Ava, but it's too deep, too masculine to be her. I don't need to turn around to know exactly who the voice belongs to.

"Robert," I say his name, nodding. "What are you doing here?"

It hasn't been even a whole day. How did he know we were here, in this exact hospital?

He approaches me, wearing shoes that squeal against the linoleum floor. His hands are in the pockets of his coat.

"The mogul of Emerald Price was kidnapped, and the doctors are fighting for his life," he informs me, as if I don't already know all this. "It took the press exactly three hours to find out and put it up online."

"Shit," I frown, losing all desire for the coffee I'm still holding in my hand. "Ava is in the waiting room, down the hall."

"I'm glad you're both alright," he tells me. "But that's actually not why I'm here."

"Why are you here then?" I wonder, taking another sip, then completely changing my mind and throwing the whole thing into the nearest trashcan.

"I'm here to see your father," he admits, looking down at his feet. "You see, what I didn't tell you was that we used to be very good friends. Best friends even. But when that whole tragic thing happened, I... I knew I couldn't stay friends with him any longer. His very face would remind me of what we could have prevented. And I didn't want such a reminder in my life."

"Now you do?"

I didn't mean it to sound as accusatory as that, but I'm still exhausted from what's happened. I can't be picky about my words. My mind is too tired, too worried.

"I want to apologize to him," he admits. "I want to tell him that I shouldn't have pushed him away like I did, making him feel even guiltier about something that wasn't our fault. We could have prevented it. Maybe. I don't know. Maybe it wouldn't have changed anything. Maybe Kellan would just nod to my advice of withdrawing from the initiation, and the same thing would have happened. Who knows? What I do know is that we should have tried to be more friendly, more humane. I saw someone suffer, and I did nothing to help him. That is my own guilt. I'm not guilty for murdering that young man, but my own guilt, which has been following me my entire life, is that I don't consider myself a good man. I'm here to tell Reinier that we shouldn't have been so hard on ourselves."

I sigh. I don't want to tell him that he might not get the chance to say any of that. I'm still waiting to hear if my father is out of the woods, but apparently, they'll only know when, and if, he wakes up. I try to think positively, but in light of everything that's happened, it's hard. Still, one look at Ava is enough to bring back all the strength I need for both of us.

"Why don't you come back to the waiting room with me?" I suggest. "And you can wait with us for the news."

"Would you mind?" He asks, and I see it in his eyes that he will accept whatever choice I deal him. Honestly, I think my father would also benefit from seeing him. This has gone on long enough. Too many lives have been lost and almost ruined.

"No," I smile. "Come on."

When we reach the waiting room, I see that Ava is already up, and the nurse is right by her side, telling her something.

"Oh, he's here," Ava points at me, and the nurse turns around.

"Mr. Price," the nurse smiles, and immediately, I feel like the whole weight of the world has just been lifted off my back. "Your father has regained consciousness. He reacted very well to the surgery, and the odds of his full recovery are very optimistic."

My heart is so full of joy I feel like it's about to burst.

"Could we go see him now, please?"

"All three of you?" The nurse looks concerned.

"I'll stay behind," Ava offers. She's seen her father the moment he walked over with me, but it seems she's only now truly registered his presence here. "Dad? What are you doing here?"

"I'd like to speak to Reinier, if possible," he addresses the nurse.

She still seems a bit apprehensive about there being more people involved in this short visit. "Just the two of you?" She asks for confirmation. I nod. "Well, alright, but do make it quick. And please, do not excite him, if possible."

I'm tempted to urge Robert to leave it for some other time, and not now when my father just got out of surgery, but perhaps it'll be good for my dad to hear what Robert has to say.

"We'll be in and out in a minute," I promise, with a dutiful nod.

"Alright then," she repeats. "Please, follow me."

We do as she instructs, following her down the still empty hallway, on the way there passing by a few more nurses and a doctor. They all seem hurried, focused on their work, not even noticing us. We stop in front of room 212. The nurse opens the door, and immediately, the heavy smell of cleaning products and steady beeping fills my nostrils and my ears. My father is lying neatly tucked in the hospital bed, with an IV hanging by his right side, connected to his vein. His head is slightly turned to the left side, the side he always preferred to sleep on, even while mom was alive.

"If he fell asleep again, please do not wake him," the nurse urges us politely.

"Thank you," I nod silently, and she leaves us.

Robert and I stand a bit awestruck before the bed, neither of us willing to take the first step in approaching my father, who lies almost reverently there. His eye is still swollen shut, and there is a butterfly plaster on his cracked lip. Just when I think he's dozed off again, and we should just let him be, his eye pops open.

"Gabe?" He whispers.

I immediately rush over to his side, grabbing him by the hand, which feels so old and worn out, like a broken branch. That isn't the hand I remember as a kid, the hand that lifted me up to reach the highest branches of a tree picking apples or to carry me on his back.

"I'm here, dad," I say, patting his hand gently. "You made it."

"Bare... ly..." He reminds me, and almost smiles.

His eye then wanders from me to Robert, when it suddenly bulges to such an extent that I fear it'll pop out of its socket.

"Rob?" He calls out with the same whisper, but this time, it is more desperate, more unbelieving.

"It's me, Reiner," Robert nods, walking over to the other side of the bed. "I heard what happened."

My father doesn't speak. I notice his swallow heavily, as his Adam's apple bobs up then back down.

"It's been a while, huh?" Robert asks, obviously feeling nervous. Maybe he's even regretting coming here. But now he's here, and he needs to say what he came to say. "Maybe this isn't the right moment, or maybe it's exactly the right moment, I don't know. I just know that when I heard what happened, I felt an urge to come down here and see you. The whole story leaked, and the press already knows it's Kellan's brother. You can get the whole story online, as if it happened yesterday."

I wonder if for both of them, it truly does feel like it happened yesterday, because for them, it's a story that changed the course of their lives. Had it not been for Kellan's death, I bet they would have stayed friends, maybe even best friends as they used to be. Maybe mine and Ava's lives would be completely different.

"You... think... it's... our... fault?" My father asks, taking a long break between each word.

Robert sighs, lifting his head up to the ceiling, then lowering his gaze back at my father. "I thought that for a very long time. Not in the sense that we caused that boy's death, but in the sense that we could have prevented it. I've seen the look of terror in his eyes when we explained what he needed to do. And you..." He hesitates, as if he thinks it might not be a good idea to continue. Then, he does, nonetheless. "You closed the lid to that coffin. You were the last man to see him alive. You can't tell me that he looked OK when you were doing that."

I look at my father. His lip is trembling.

"We could have prevented it, Reinier, and we didn't," he says again, echoing his conviction. "I understand his brother's need for revenge. But that is just what life is sometimes. It's unfair. I mean, why are there so many hungry people in the world? Why do kids end up getting hurt in a drive by shooting? They were just in the wrong place at the wrong time. Sometimes, that is all that's needed for your life to take a completely wrong turn. It took me a long time to understand that's exactly what happened. That young man didn't deserve to die. Especially not in that way. But he did. And it was a tragedy. It still is. However, we can't keep blaming ourselves for the what ifs of other people. Life is unfair. We need to accept it as such, otherwise... there is nothing left..."

My father presses his lips together, in an effort to pacify his tremors, but it's impossible. I notice his other hand beckoning at Robert to come closer. Robert approaches him. My father's fingers are still calling out to him, and after a few moments of hesitation, they join hands.

"We... need... forgiveness..." My father says. All Robert can do is nod. "From... ourselves..." My father adds, and this is where a tear rolls down his cheek.

I've never seen my father cry. Not even when my mother died. He locked himself in his study for a whole day after her funeral, and my aunt took care of me the following week. When I asked her where he was, she said he was busy getting his business affairs in order in his study. For a long time, I believed that to be true. I wondered how he could just keep on with his life, without her. Then suddenly, I realized he was getting wasted for days. Drinking during the day, sleeping during the night, for a whole week. Then, he got out of his study, and this was the person that emerged out of that room, the person I knew until now.

Suddenly, a knock is heard, and the door opens, with that same nurse popping up.

"I'm sorry, but Mr. Price really needs to rest now," she urges.

"Of course," Robert nods first, letting go of my father's hand.

"Hold on, dad," I smile at him. "We'll come visit you tomorrow, Ava and I."

This time, he manages a smile. When I reach the door and turn around for another look, he's already fallen asleep. Maybe that is how one sleeps with an unburdened conscience.

We walk out and close the door silently behind us. Ava is waiting. Maybe we could go back to my place and freshen up. God knows it's been a helluva week.

Chapter Twenty-Five

Ava

"Come on!" I shout after Gabriel, slightly annoyed. He obviously wants to show off that he's faster than me, and I'm too tired to keep up. "We've been walking for three hours! Are we there yet?"

This was his surprise. He just picked me up this morning, saying there is a special place he wants to take me to. I figured, it was a special restaurant or maybe a museum. Then he told me to wear comfortable clothes. OK. Some minor walking tour. But there is nothing minor about trekking in the mountains. OK. We didn't climb very high up, but we are still walking a lot, and someone like me who's a bit out of shape, would really appreciate a short rest. But he keeps urging me to continue, that our destination is worth it. I believe it is. I'd just like to rest a little first before getting there.

He turns to me, his face all hopeful and sun-kissed, because it's an unusually hot September morning. Bathed in the soft sunny glow, Gabriel looks even more handsome than usual, if such a thing is even possible. I remember Sylvia's comment when we saw him that fateful night at the bar. She'd fuck him. I'd fuck him, too, I just didn't want to admit it. It turns out, she's been right about that, and about a whole array of other things. And I couldn't have been happier about it.

I'm breathing heavily, silently thanking him for being the one to carry that heavy backpack as we trekked through the forest and up the hill. He's standing a little further down the road, waiting for me. I wonder where he gets all that energy from.

"Come on, slowpoke, just a little while longer!" He shouts back at me.

"Easy for you to say," I mumble, managing to catch up to him somehow.

"What do you think?" He asks me, and only then do I realize what he is showing me.

The view behind him is absolutely breath-taking. In the midst of all that lush greenery, there is a disc of the brightest blue color. The sun is bathing in it like in a mirror, reflecting the clouds and the clear sky above us. I feel in awe of the sight before me. I don't remember ever seeing anything this pure. It feels like I've seen this place somewhere, maybe in my dreams, without even being aware of it.

"It's beautiful, isn't it?" He asks.

I take a few steps closer, admiring the lake. I see it shine all the shades of blue and green, cyan, turquoise. In the distance, the hills surround it like giant protectors, keeping this gem hidden from the rest of the world. Only those who know what they are looking for can actually find it. That is the beauty of such places.

"It's beyond beautiful," I agree, feeling as if nature truly is the most talented painter, creating the most impossible wonders with its brush.

Gabriel seems to be reading my mind. "Can you see all those colors?"

"Mhm," I nod.

"Those are the colors that will never fade," he whispers. "Just like my love for you."

I turn to him, my heart feeling as if it's about to jump out of my chest. "This is the most beautiful place for a picnic you could have chosen."

"It's actually not me who found this heaven on earth," he says, stepping behind me and wrapping his arms around my waist. "It was my mother."

Then, it hits me. This is the lake he was telling his father about when we were at that warehouse, fighting for his father's life. This was the lake that kept his father alive. This lake and the memories that it has created for them as a family. The thought that he would bring me here to share this special place with me fills me with love the likes of which I never thought I could ever feel for a man.

"She sounds like an angel," I say.

"She was before, and she is now," he says sadly, and I bite my tongue for choosing the wrong word when any other could have worked much better.

"You know, this place is making me feel like she is still here, in a way," he whispers right into my ear, his gaze focused somewhere in the distance, at the lake.

"She's not just here," I correct him, trying to catch that same spot in the distance, but I know I can't it belongs only to him. "She is everywhere you go, because she lives inside your heart. The memory if of her is what's keeping her alive."

"She would really like you, you know that?" He grins.

"You think so?" I beam with pride.

"She was also into that hippie shit," he chuckles. I join in. "But you know I love it. Come on now, let's set up the picnic."

He lets me go, and together, we take out the picnic blanket, setting it up right by the lake. I am tempted to go for a swim, but despite its crystal clarity, or maybe exactly because of it, the lake feels like ice. If I swim in it, I might end up with a pneumonia, so it's better not to risk it. Instead, I help Gabriel with the picnic blanket. We set up the sandwiches, the lemonade, the thermos with two cups for the coffee.

"Wait a second," he suddenly gets up just when I thought that we set up everything and we could start eating. After three hours of walking and him saying just fifteen minutes more for six times, I'm downright ravenous.

"OK," I agree, curious as to what more he could possibly need.

I watch him run away, lowering down to the earth a few times, and picking something. When he finally returns, he's holding a miniature bouquet of wildflowers.

"Are those for me?" I beam.

"No, don't be silly," he pretends to frown, but his reply is so funny I burst out into laughter even before he continues. "These are for the picnic."

"But I'm here for the picnic, too," I tease.

"Not everything is for you," he sticks his tongue out at me.

"Watch out, I bite, you know," I reply playfully.

"I'm counting on that, honey," he winks at me, as he sets the flowers in a circle in the middle of the blanket. "Now, what do you think?"

I look at the flower arrangement, at the set up plates, the food, the drink. Then, I look at the two of us. The love I feel for this man is overwhelming. Sometimes, I dare not even admit it to myself. But I've learned one thing, and that is to just let go and enjoy the moment, like this one right now. Whatever moment we are in, can be the perfect moment. All we need to do is be in it.

"Are you OK?" He asks, looking at me strangely.

"Yeah, why?" I smile.

"You seem lost in thought somehow."

"I am," I admit. "But I'm back here with you now. I promise. You've brought me to this beautiful place, and I want you to know how thrilled I am to be here."

"That's good, because I have a confession to make," he grins, scratching the back of his neck.

"A confession?" I cloud up. I don't know why, but I immediately think of something bad. He did something bad, and he needed to bring me to this wonderful place, so I wouldn't be as mad as I would have been somewhere else.

Stop overthinking things. That little voice inside of me reminds me of the truth of my condition. I do always tend to overthink things. I should hear him out first, and then see whether it's something to get upset about.

Oh, God, I hope not.

"I brought you here with a specific reason in mind," he says almost ceremoniously, getting up. His hand dives into his pocket, and extracts a small, royal blue box, which fits perfectly in the palm of his hand. I watch as he goes down to one knee, extending the hand with the box in it.

"Gabriel..." I say his name, feeling a tidal wave of emotion wash over me. I can't think straight. All I see is him down on his knee, and I know that can mean only one thing. "What are you doing?" I smile awkwardly, and all I want to do is giggle, as I do when I'm extremely nervous.

"I'm taking the craziest risk of my entire life," he says, adjusting himself on his knee, so that he's perfectly balanced now. "There we go." He adds, and I almost burst out into nervous laughter. Still, I manage to remain calm, anticipating his next words. "I know we can't say that we've known each other for years, like other couples do. Compared to them, we're just babies, in that department. Wait, babies? That's not what I planned on saying," he shakes his head, slapping himself on the forehead with his open palm.

This is the moment where I can't resist laughing. "Sorry, I'm sorry..." I wave my hands apologetically at him. "I don't mean to laugh at your proposal. It's cute. You're cute."

"You know, this isn't easy at all," he pouts theatrically at me, pretending to be upset. "How about you try to do it?"

"Me?" I wonder. "Sure."

I jump and grab the box from his hand. He is shocked that I accepted the dare so quickly. His other knee drops to the blanket, and he's sitting now, with me on one knee before him. Strangely, I don't feel awkward at all. This feels like the most natural stance in the world, and that little box in my hand is exactly where it needs to be.

"Gabriel," I start ceremoniously, "I know that we haven't known each other for very long. At least, not as long as other would have expected us to, as we are on the threshold to this momentous change—"

"Threshold?" He winks at me. "Nice."

"Shhh," I scold him playfully. "I'm proposing here." He pretends to zip up his mouth, then nods for me to continue. "Thank you. Now, where was I? Oh yes. On the threshold to this momentous change. But I feel like in this short amount of time, we truly saw each other's soul. We gazed deeply into it, and we saw each other's essences, which in turn, recognized each other. We belong together. We are soul mates. And the amount of time necessary to establish that doesn't matter, because we will have the rest of our lives to reassure each other of that fact, every single morning upon waking and every single evening upon falling asleep. So, Gabriel Price, would you do me the honor of marrying me?"

The question lingers in the air, as he says nothing. He is just staring at me, as if he's seeing me truly for the first time, and he can't take his eyes off ofoff me.

"Gabe?" I smile. "Hello?"

"Yes," he nods, wrapping his arms around me, and standing up, only to swirl me high up into the air. "Yes, yes, a thousand times yes!"

I put my hands on his shoulders, giggling. "I thought this was just pretend."

"None of this was pretend," he corrects me. "This was actually my plan all along, making you do it. Now, you've asked me to marry you, I said yes, and it's a done deal. You can't back down now."

He lowers me to the ground and takes the box from my hand. When he opens it, I see a beautiful pear-shaped diamond, with a starburst of little diamonds around it. It is dainty, yet delicate. I have no idea how he knew exactly the kind of ring I wanted it, but he got it.

"This ring is a binding contract," he announces, taking my hand, as the ring hovers at the very tip of my ring finger. "If you say yes, then you will be mine to love and to hold forever. In life and in death. If that is what you want."

I slide my finger into the whole, settling the ring on my finger. "I can't think of wanting anything else in the world this much."

I cup his face with my hands and bring my lips to his. Neither of us wants to pull away first. We both feel as if this kiss is the first true kiss of the rest of our lives. Forgiveness has brought us this far. Love will take us the rest of the way.

*****

Don't miss out!

Visit the website below and you can sign up to receive emails whenever Erica Frost publishes a new book. There's no charge and no obligation.

https://books2read.com/r/B-A-YRSV-NYZCC

BOOKS 2 READ

Connecting independent readers to independent writers.

Also by Erica Frost

Seduced By A Billionaire
Dark Secrets
A Billionaire's Game
Power Play
Ruthless Rival
Taming The Billionaire
The Hated Billionaire
3-Pointer